Short
Circuit

Short Circuit

Laurence Oriol

Translated from the French by W. G. Corp

THE WORLD PUBLISHING COMPANY
CLEVELAND AND NEW YORK

Published by The World Publishing Company
2231 West 110th Street, Cleveland, Ohio 44102
First World Printing 1968

First published in the French language in 1966
under the title *L'Interne de Service* by Editions Denoël,
14 rue Amélie, Paris 7e.
© 1966 by Editions Denoël, Paris
This translation © Macdonald & Co. (Publishers) Ltd., 1967
First published in Great Britain by
Macdonald & Co. (Publishers) Ltd.
© 1968 by The World Publishing Company

Library of Congress Catalog Card Number: 68–19331

PRINTED IN THE UNITED STATES OF AMERICA

I

The room—some sixteen feet by thirteen—had white walls and a large window with a balcony. It contained a brass bedstead, a wardrobe, an old oak chest of drawers, a bedside table and two chairs.

The victim looked the same as anyone else who had died a violent death—at least to Commissaire Faure who had never quite accustomed himself to the sight.

A cigarette hanging from his thick lips, the police doctor stated that death was due to electrocution and had occurred some twelve or thirteen hours previously. When the body had been found it was already too late to attempt resuscitation. Burned hands, livid face. Nothing else of any importance to report at the moment. That being so, could the body now be removed?

Faure nodded. His almost completely bald head barely reached the shoulder of Inspector Rageot who was standing beside him, hands in pockets, shifting his weight from one foot to the other, and looking at nothing in particular. Rageot had arrived at the same time as the police doctor and the identification service—a good half-hour before the commissaire.

"Let's get on with it, then," said Faure. "I'm in a hurry. A domestic crisis."

"Nothing serious, I hope?"

The commissaire made a vague gesture, taking the opportunity to glance at his wristwatch.

"Right!" said Rageot. "First: as in every bedroom in this

5

place, the bedstead is brass—an excellent conductor—and the flooring is tiles. Second: the wires of the bedside lamp had been tampered with near the switch. Third: nothing was left to chance—that's to say, the victim had no hope whatever of escaping. Come and look . . . there . . . behind the bed . . . the beading which covers the electrical circuit. You'll have to bend down. Now d'you see? Close to the left leg of the bed the beading is broken—almost five inches is missing. That's what put me on the track. Someone must have pulled a wire out from this circuit and attached it to the bed-leg. But to get the current to pass, a second wire had to be fixed to a different part of the bed and joined up to one of the lamp terminals. The circuit was then completed by linking the other lamp terminal to the mains supply. D'you follow? In electricity it's called a series connection. Believe me, it's the best possible way to arrange an electrocution. Fixed this way, the victim has only to touch any part of the bed-frame to receive the full charge. A dead cert, if I may use the expression."

The two men straightened up, red in the face. Faure lit another cigarette, glanced at his watch again, and asked: "Have you found the wires which were used?"

"Someone got rid of them before the police arrived. The author of this little trick, no doubt," Rageot replied.

He was a fair-haired man with fat cheeks and a comic, very short, turned-up nose.

"All the same, we can't rule out the possibility of its being an accident," said Faure absently.

"If this was an accident, I'm Brigitte Bardot. Seriously, it's as plain as the nose on my face. D'you want me to give you a demonstration? Shall I show you just how a series connection is fixed? It won't take five minutes."

"The experts can deal with that. In any case, I can't bear fiddling with electric points."

"Listen," persisted Rageot. "If we don't accept the series connection hypothesis, only the bared wire of the bedside lamp could have been the cause of an accident; but in that case there'd just have been a short-circuit. So, to sum up,

6

this series wiring was carried out with criminal intent. There's ample proof under your nose. At the spot where the beading was removed, one wire is bare; and the wires of the bedside lamp have been bared, too. Look."

They crossed to the bedside table and Rageot bent over the lamp. Faure, his mind elsewhere, said hurriedly: "Fine, fine. I'm sure you're right. Have the lamp taken in."

Rageot, straightening up, glanced at the commissaire in surprise. The domestic crisis must be a serious one. He lit a cigarette before returning to his hypothesis.

"Anyone could have done an amateurish job like this. It's probably described in some Beginner's Guide to Murder. The lack of finesse makes me want to burst into tears. There's nothing very clever about making a series connection and removing the incriminating wires if you leave the marks, clear, obvious and undeniable. I'd say it was a woman's work, if I may make the suggestion."

"You may not," said Faure. "Where's the lieutenant?"

"Here," announced a loud voice from the landing.

The *lieutenant de gendarmerie* came into the room grinning. He was tall and fat, with pink cheeks and ferrety eyes that sparkled with apparently tireless gaiety. As the victim had died in Chantilly, he had been the first person to be notified. It was he who, rejecting the possibility of an accident, had got in touch immediately with the *Sûreté Nationale*. He thought he had a pretty good idea of what had happened and would like to know the commissaire's opinion. Did he think . . . ?

No, Faure had no opinion and for the time being he didn't want to form one. He would have to clear the whole business up when the routine work had been completed. The request to go to Chantilly had come at a most inconvenient time. His youngest daughter was running a high temperature which might mean anything. The doctor had prescribed antibiotics, but Faure was sure this was a mistake; his three other children had never been able to tolerate antibiotics, and the youngest was sure to react in the same way. She would be in a terrible state by the evening, and her mother, who was neurotic anyway, would become impossible. He'd have a fine old time trying to nurse his daughter and calm his wife at the same time. Anyway, he intended to try to expedite some of the routine work.

Walking towards the room where the witnesses were waiting, he stopped suddenly and looked again at his watch. Rageot, who was watching him, noticed the dark rings under his eyes, his grey face and his unusually preoccupied expression.

"What's up now?"

"Look," said Faure, "you're old enough to do the questioning. How many are there?"

"Three, not counting the old servant and her husband. In any case, they live in the small bungalow at the far end of the garden. They saw nothing and heard nothing. The poor old dears are scared out of their wits. There's nothing much to be got out of them for the moment."

"Try all the same. In any case, I want to see the other three at the *Sûreté* tomorrow. As they all live in Paris there shouldn't be any difficulty. Well, that's that. I'm off. Ring me later this evening at home. I'm sure to be in . . . unfortunately!"

He left the house, and, walking towards his car, saw a fat, plain girl with a flushed face approaching him.

"Excuse me . . . could you tell me . . . could you tell me . . . You *are* the police, aren't you?"

He nodded, opened the door of his Floride convertible, and said:

"Well? What do you want to know?"

"The name of the victim."

As he slid into his seat, Faure, thinking of what awaited him at home, answered abruptly:

"*I'm* the victim—as always. Make no mistake about that."

A group photograph, fifteen inches by ten. The striking face of a young man of about twenty stood out from among a score of others.

He had sat composedly in front of the camera, disregarding

8

both the broad-shouldered man on his left and the girl with fair lank hair who was seen only in profile because she had turned towards him.

He was the only one of this group of resident and non-resident medical students grouped round their professor who had thought to smile. The smile suited him. But anything would suit him. He was a quite remarkably good-looking young man.

That was what Commissaire Faure was thinking as he sat at his desk, a cigarette between two fingers of his right hand and the fifteen-by-ten photograph in his left. He was thinking at the same time of his holiday in Brittany. Normally he took it in July, but this year it was to be postponed *sine die*.

Three weeks. An all-time record for slowness in a case which had at the outset seemed so straightforward: electrocution, murder, *cherchez la femme*.

There it was. His mistake had been to think that jealousy could have been the motive for the murder. These people, the principal witnesses, had been jealous only of their own reputations. Yet God knows they were shameless enough. They called it being frank—"I want to be perfectly frank . . . speaking absolutely frankly . . ."—as if they had nothing but frankness to worry about, as if they must at all costs confess their dirty little sins. However, despite this orgy of frankness, Faure had not yet discovered which of the three suspects had, one evening in May, clumsily tampered with an electrical circuit for a very definite purpose.

It was pointless to look beyond the three of them. One must be the murderer. The old servant and her husband, who had been completely ruled out, had stated that during the twenty-four hours before the murder nobody had entered the house at Chantilly.

As he put the photograph away in the file, Faure thought of Inspector Rageot. He had done a very efficient job. He had cross-examined all the secondary witnesses very carefully. This evidence alone allowed one to reconstitute step by step the outrageous intentions of one of the suspects. Rageot had

9

also unearthed the private diary of the victim. There, too, was an orgy of frankness; but could one entirely trust those hurriedly scribbled pages that reflected so consuming an obsession?

Faure lay back in his chair and passed an elegant hand across his weary face. He grimaced, as he did each time he re-examined this file. He had there the complete story of four people, including the victim, who had been involved in the same drama. What puzzled him most was the way that all the testimonies, which should at some point have shown a contradiction, tallied perfectly. The wall of dissimulation seemed to have no crack. Everyone had stated his case with an absurd frankness that probably concealed some simple truth.

As he consulted his notes, it suddenly occurred to Faure that he had not so far considered the drama as a whole. He had looked at it from the angle of each of the four protagonists. It needed a producer. This presented no insuperable difficulty—it would probably be necessary to adjust the various statements patiently, as one moves the pieces of a jigsaw puzzle—but it would be a laborious job, and, above all, tedious.

He closed the file with a sigh, and stood up. It was ten past six. If he went home now he wouldn't be able to work or even to think. During the past few days his wife's neurotic symptoms had grown worse: she couldn't speak three words without bursting into tears, and she made scenes on the slightest provocation. As for the children. . . . Well, obviously the children were suffering the consequences of having a neurotic mother. Faure was cowardly enough to put his own responsibility for this state of affairs out of his mind.

He was about to put on his jacket, but changed his mind and replaced it on the coat-rack. As he sat down again at his desk he wondered if he ought to telephone his wife. He hesitated for a moment, then decided he wasn't in the mood to listen to her reproaches. He wouldn't ring her.

It was a quarter past six when he reopened the file.

2

It all began for Danielle Fellegrini one afternoon in November when she met Guillaume Brassart.

She soon knew where she was with him. He was six-foot-two, with broad shoulders and a paunch he could no longer conceal. In medical circles he was known as the Great B. He had been a surgeon and a *professeur agrégé* for a number of years, years which had passed too quickly for his liking. He was now pushing fifty, and this was the only fact which caused him concern.

Danielle, too, was concerned about the passing of time. She was much younger than Guillaume—only thirty-two—but was one of those natural redheads who fade rather quickly, one of the dainty redheads whom men find briefly attractive. She was afraid she was going to find herself completely alone, with only the small resources she had in a savings-bank, and small chance of a suitable husband, or even a lover.

She had worked most of her life, but without enthusiasm or ambition . . . without conviction. She could type and she spoke a schoolgirl English which nobody could understand, least of all the English. But she was pretty. When she met Guillaume she was an airport hostess at Orly, a job which soon began to interfere disastrously with their meetings, for her new lover had a well-established leisure-pattern which rarely coincided with her own.

This led him to suggest that she should give up her job. He would, he said, let her have an allowance equivalent to her salary.

"How much do you get?"

"I don't want to be a kept woman."

Unsmilingly she told him that the wretched end of the heroine of *Back Street* had a traumatic effect on her. She had no wish, if he died before she did or simply left her, to finish her life in a shabby hotel with a mangy little dog as her sole companion. In short, she didn't want his money and would rather work. Work offered more security.

Guillaume found this both baffling and intolerable. He was not used to pleading for what he wanted and to do so now he had put on a little-boy face.

"You wouldn't be a kept woman. I'd give you a monthly allowance which would be just like the housekeeping money any husband gives his wife."

Danielle lived in an atrociously furnished one-roomed flat, which had been her home for the past ten years. It was modern and uncomfortable. The rugs looked like sample pieces of the cheap carpets mass-produced in North Africa. Guillaume's eyes wandered over the pink and blue walls, the sagging easy chairs, and the whitewood chest-of-drawers that had been clumsily overpainted.

Absurdly moved, he said quickly: "I really do love you. You must believe me."

"Would you marry me?"

"If it was possible, yes."

Fortunately for him, he thought, it was not. He explained to her that his wife was a devout Catholic who would never give him a divorce.

"Suppose she was forced to?"

"Even if my wife agreed to a divorce—which is highly unlikely—her father would ruin me. He's a very powerful man."

"Then there's no point going on talking about it. You stay with your wife, and I'll apply for a transfer. I've been offered a better job at Nice Airport. I should have to leave here in a month from now."

He was furious. No one in the past ten years had ever questioned any decision he made, either at the hospital or at home, and now this little piece . . . but he couldn't do without the little piece. It was absurd, it was completely idiotic, but it was true, he realized during the week when he didn't see her. By the time they met again he was much more conciliatory.

"I've been thinking a great deal about you. What seemed impossible to me last week can probably be arranged. It'll be a long, difficult business, and risky, very risky; but I think I may have found a solution."

That same evening he talked to her for the first time about Vincent Debosse. The next day she decided to give up work.

For Guillaume, it all started one day in January as the result of a foolish impulse. He hadn't mentioned Vincent Debosse to Danielle again for a month.

Opening a drawer of his desk just before he left the hospital he had happened to see a fifteen-by-ten photograph that had been taken of his department a few days earlier. Thinking it might please Danielle to see him lording it in his white coat over his young assistants, he took it with him to show her that evening. By the time he realized he had made a colossal blunder it was too late to do anything to remedy his mistake.

"Debosse is the one who's smiling, isn't he?"

It would have been futile to deny it. She wouldn't have believed him.

"That's right."

He stretched out on the settee, realizing that his evening and even his night were probably going to be spoiled.

For a whole month he had felt very pleased with himself. He had his life perfectly organized: twice a week, each Tuesday and Friday, he dined with Danielle and remained with her all night. Although she did talk occasionally about things improving later on, she seemed quite satisfied with the present situation. Now this incident looked like upsetting everything.

She was standing by the table, still staring at the photograph.

"He looks very young," she remarked.

Then she glanced at Guillaume who was no longer young.

13

His face was lined and blotchy, and he had the nose of a prize-fighter.

"Very young? I shouldn't have thought so. Twenty-six or seven. He stoops badly. . . . Oh, for heaven's sake, don't be childish! Give me back the photo."

"You hate him, don't you!"

"Possibly. I'd never given the matter a thought. Give me back the photo. He's too subservient, too much of a schemer for my liking."

"He's good-looking."

"Yes, he's good-looking."

"Just the man we need."

He looked at her silently for a moment, both furious and dumbfounded. It was disagreeable to have something he had relegated to the back of his mind brought to the fore again. He had naturally assumed that Danielle, too, had . . .

"You're not going to start thinking about all that again, are you?"

"I've never stopped thinking about it."

She took a magnifying-glass from the chest-of-drawers, and held it close to the photograph, looking for the umpteenth time at the smiling face around which she was building an equally smiling future for herself.

"Blue eyes?"

"I really don't know."

"A short, straight nose. A dimpled chin."

"Are you really enjoying this conversation?"

"It's important."

Guillaume stared at her. Beautiful legs, and a slim, supple body which he would soon be holding in his arms. That was what he'd come for. Since the first time he met her, that was what he'd gone on wanting. He thought he could never tire of it.

"What are you thinking about?"

"My wife."

She put the photograph on the table and, though she was only two steps away, looked at him as remotely as she might look at a loaded revolver. Thinking this was probably one of her bad days, he decided he must be patient and diplomatic, and tell more lies than usual.

"Tell me about your wife."

"You know as much about her as I do."

"I've never even seen her."

"You've spied on her plenty of times through our windows. You even followed her into a tea-room one afternoon."

"How do you know that?"

"I do know."

He tried to pull her on to the settee, but she refused. He sighed.

"What is it you want?"

"Oh, nothing! Nothing of any importance. Something very trivial . . . something that's known as happiness."

He shrugged and began rubbing the bridge of his nose— his favourite tic. He had been right, but not only was this one of her bad days, she was setting her sights altogether too high. Happiness! Had he ever asked himself whether he was happy or unhappy? He had never had time. There was his work, and, apart from that, the few pleasures which life could offer . . . holding Danielle in his arms, for instance.

"It's a bit miserable here," he said, trying to sound conciliatory. "Why don't you get another flat? I've offered hundreds of times to give you a new one. You want somewhere larger and brighter, without all this ridiculous furniture . . . and, above all, in a part of Paris which would be more convenient for me."

"That's not the problem. What are you going to do about Debosse?"

"Nothing. Nothing at all. Forget him! Completely!"

She turned pale and suddenly felt very cold. Her world was collapsing around her and she stood there, transfixed, not yet entirely believing what she had heard.

For a month she had been daydreaming because Guillaume himself had held out this lifeline to her. God alone knew what she had been dreaming of . . . a life of comfort, a life without problems, a life of happiness. Being able to dream of future

15

happiness had alone enabled her to endure the thankless role she was at present playing in Guillaume's life, and now, suddenly, with a snap of his fingers, a single sentence, he had sent her whole imagined future tumbling in ruin. Draw a neat line. The dream has ended. What lies ahead is real life—short, hopeless, unbearable.

Suddenly she made up her mind that no matter what it might cost her, she wasn't going to put up with that sort of life.

"You'd better go now," she said, without raising her voice. "I'm not stopping you."

She saw his expression of incredulity and his big hand stubbing out a cigarette. Then she saw nothing more. He had leapt to his feet and, seizing her by the elbows, held her facing him. She lowered her eyes. He told her rapidly that tricks like that wouldn't work with him, he was neither a monk nor a half-wit, he wasn't leaving and she'd better get that straight. Then he sat down again.

Taking a crumpled cigarette from the packet in his pocket, he added that he was quite willing to listen to what she had to say, even if she was determined only to reproach him. He had plenty of time.

"Plenty of time," thought Danielle. "That's just what I haven't got." She had to act quickly . . . very quickly. But she felt a fool. Stupid.

She pushed an armchair into place opposite Guillaume and sat down in it, crossing her legs.

"This man, Debosse," she said. "I didn't invent him. It was you who talked to me about him a month ago. I remember it quite clearly. I handed in my notice the next day and gave up work. You told me . . ."

"I told you that he was very good-looking, very poor, very ambitious, and that someone like him—if one handled it right—would stick at nothing. That's all. Well, I was wrong."

"That's not all and you know it. And you weren't wrong."

"It was a crazy idea, and I'm not a complete fool. Can I have a whisky?"

"Get it yourself."

She watched him walk towards the kitchen, a massive, age-ing figure. She realized she no longer loved him, that possibly she had never loved him; but that was an added reason for obliging him to marry her. A crazy idea? It had been his own idea. She would never have dreamed of such a thing, but she would be out of her mind if she forgot all about it now. It was her last chance. She, Danielle Fellegrini, was going to grasp this slim chance of becoming Madame Brassart—with the help of young Debosse.

"Whisky?"

She raised her eyes, saw that he was holding out a glass, and shook her head. She noticed he had already drained his own.

"You drink too much."

"I drink because it helps me to listen to you.   Now, are you going to talk, or shall I?"

"No one's going to talk. No one's ever going to try to make me believe crazy ideas again. Tomorrow I shall go and get another job, and now I'd be obliged if you'd leave me. I want to be alone."

"Are you joking?"

"Do I look as if I'm joking?"

She stood up, facing him, her face pale, dark shadows under her extraordinarily green eyes. She was a head shorter than he was, standing erect, her eyes on his trembling lips.

"What are you after?"

She shrugged her shoulders, waved one long, slender arm as if to brush away a fly. He knew perfectly well what she was after.

"You mean that idea about Debosse?"

The same shrug of the shoulders, the same wave of her arm, but directed this time towards the hall. Guillaume lifted his head to say "no", as if he were too moved for words, then, suddenly, he swung his hand with a dry crack against Danielle's cheek.

He could not see that she was smiling, nor that there was an unmistakable gleam of triumphant amusement in her eyes. She had turned her head away too quickly for him to see her

17

reaction, and had run towards the bathroom. He assumed she wanted to hide her tears.

As he pulled on his overcoat, he reflected that this was all so stupid. A whole evening spoiled. Ought he to stay, and try to patch things up? But he didn't dare go to her. Sitting on the arm of a chair, he waited. He thought about the situation, which was ridiculous, and about the precious time that he—the Great B—was being forced to waste. He thought, too, how much he had changed since the days when he used to corner any reasonably pretty nurse or female student in the operating theatre of the hospital. None of them had ever dared to protest. Sometimes they had even seemed to enjoy it.

It was always after a particularly difficult operation that he felt the need to make love—for ten minutes or a quarter of an hour at most. He never looked after them as they left—some, no doubt, with heads hanging and tears in their eyes, some smiling triumphantly, only too eager to rush off and tell their story to the others. He realized that the next day everyone in the hospital probably knew what had happened, but this caused him no concern at all. He persuaded himself that this behaviour added a picturesque footnote to his reputation as a great fellow.

He did not even care if he offended his father-in-law, Professor Gladieux. The Professor, who had now retired, covered with honour and glory, had been his own chief. It was for him that he had made the sacrifice of becoming a Catholic, the price he was required to pay for the hand of Mademoiselle Gladieux.

This, however, was the only concession he had ever made to a woman. After his marriage he had continued to amuse himself with the nurses and girl students. It was in the operating theatre that he felt at home. Only there did he feel really alive. Hence, perhaps, his imperious desire to make love there. In what others thought of—wrongly—as his home, the flat in the Place Malesherbes where he had lived for twenty years, there was his wife who bored him to distraction, and his two sons who had, as children, scrambled over him when he wished them elsewhere, and whom he had caressed awkwardly from time to time because he didn't like children and didn't know how to talk to them.

Now there was Danielle, someone unique in his life as a man. Since he had known her, the nurses and students in his department had found themselves left unexpectedly in peace. He told himself that perhaps he loved her, that this infatuation was, possibly, love. Was Danielle intelligent, or simply tenacious and artful? He didn't know. It was a type of question that had virtually never arisen in his relations with women. They were either pretty and easy, which was all he asked of them, or they were plain and therefore didn't exist for him.

When Danielle reappeared, he had been waiting for twenty minutes. She said "Still there?" without surprise or anger, and walked past the table into the hall, where she threw a coat over her shoulders.

"Are you going out?"

He scarcely recognized his own voice, it was so hollow and anxious. He felt very foolish.

"Yes. That is, if you don't leave."

He realized that it was useless to insist. He might as well bang his head against a stone wall. It occurred to him that this might be no more than a capricious mood, or even a trick, but he wasn't used to playing games with women. He didn't know the rules, nor did he wish to learn. The Great B had no time for that sort of thing.

As he walked past her he squeezed out a smile and said he was sorry about the silly misunderstanding. As he left he added: "See you soon."

When he had gone she gulped down the whisky he had poured out for her. She felt chilled. The photograph, which he had forgotten, still lay on the table. She put it inside the chest-of-drawers, between her lace panties and her nylon slip. She told herself that this was proper homage to Vincent Debosse, who was handsome, ambitious and poor, and whom nothing now could ever make her forget.

19

3

He lived at Asnières, on the outskirts of Paris, in a two-roomed flat with a kitchen but no bathroom. His life with his mother had been dull, but peaceful, until she died a year before from a respiratory disease. He mourned her still; she had been the only woman he had ever been able to endure.

Madame Debosse had not been a very intelligent woman, however. She had been swarthy, no beauty, without a spare ounce of flesh—her face prematurely ravaged, perhaps as a result of the heavy work she had undertaken for the sake of "my boy", for "my boy's" education, to build a future for "my boy". Vincent was a source of constant admiration to her, he was her whole world. She often wondered how she could be the mother of so marvellous a creature. She discounted the role played in his creation by his father, whom she had seen no more than two or three times before he disappeared from her life. She had never thought of trying to find him.

Since his mother's death, Vincent had lived on 250 francs a month, his salary as a non-resident medical student. His diet consisted of a large cup of cocoa and a bread roll every evening. He claimed that this was ample, that, in any case, he hated stuffing himself, that a light meal enabled him to study with greater concentration.

This particular evening, however, was exceptional because he had just learned that his own chief, the Great B, was to be a member of the board of the *Internat*. Exceptionally, therefore, Vincent had treated himself to a bottle of wine and a plate of salami. As he wasn't used to drinking he fell quickly into a state of dull, ineffectual resentment in which he brooded on the likelihood that the Great B, whom he disliked and who obviously hated him, would seize the opportunity of spoiling his chances of passing the *Internat* examination.

Vincent was sitting for the examination this year for the third time. On the first two occasions he had not even passed the written part. Then, last December, contrary to all expectations, his name had appeared on the list of candidates for the oral part. He had immediately begun to study an extra two hours every day, including Sundays. He had had no leisure for a very long time. He recalled with a certain nostalgia a film he had seen some three years earlier, a Western then some fifteen years old.

As he finished his wine he felt as if a large lump was rising in his throat, and thought he was going to cry. He stood up to clear the table, which had not been polished since his mother's death, staggered and fell over. As he clambered to his feet he found himself cursing the Great B and hospital consultants in general, and his own individual dog's life in particular.

He washed up his plate and glass in the greasy sink, and told himself that he ought to give up. He almost decided not to attend the oral examination. "It's no good, I'm beaten. I'll just settle for being a G.P. like Mother wanted."

His mother. She was smiling at him timidly from the plastic frame standing on the sideboard. He remembered her expression of bewilderment and alarm when he had told her that he probably wouldn't complete his studies for ten years. Wasn't the seven years necessary to become a doctor enough? No, the real world of medicine was in the hospitals. When he passed the *Externat* exam he would sit for the *Internat*: 4,500 pages of medicine, surgery and physiology to be learned by heart, or near enough. He would sit for the exam, but he was well aware that you didn't stand much of a chance without the backing of one of the great men. Madame Debosse couldn't understand this. Surely he was exaggerating, as usual. "Don't be silly, Mother," he had said. "They all hang together. The son of a famous consultant, or the son-in-law, or even a chap who has good connections in those sort of circles, has every chance of passing. It shouldn't be so, but it is."

For him the only chance was to work like a demon and then to succeed somehow in controlling his panic on the day of the examination.

"Panic. I'm panicking already," he muttered to himself as he lay down to sleep. His bedroom was ten feet square with a low, grimy ceiling, its walls covered with a dismal grey, daisy-patterned wallpaper.

Daisies. I love you, I love you not. Hate. "I hate that bastard, Brassart," he said to himself. Then he resolved that nothing would stop him sitting for the *Internat* examination, and settled into an uneasy sleep.

Hélène Accard, who was twenty-four, had dull, fair hair and was an external student in the Great B's department. She was in love with Vincent Debosse. She saw him arriving in the hospital courtyard, hunched-up on a dilapidated motor-cycle.

"You've got a nerve," she said. "The chief's here already."

He was wearing a shapeless green lumber-jacket over an old sports shirt, and a beret pulled down almost to his eyes.

"Even when you do your best to make yourself look ugly, you don't succeed, lovey."

"Please don't call me lovey."

She was a particularly pretty girl, but to him she was like all other women, except that she caused him more annoyance because she was always pestering him.

"What would you like me to call you?"

"Nothing. Just leave me alone."

He wrung his cold hands, reddened by the biting wind, and took off his beret. He smoothed his thick, dark hair. Hélène, who was used to such cavalier treatment, kept close to his heels.

"Have you heard the news?"

He growled "What news?" as he strode towards the door of the Lecène building. She was having to trot to keep up with him.

"Great B is to be a member of the *Internat* board."

He shot her a blue-eyed glance of annoyance.

"I know. So what?"

She pushed back the fair hair which was falling across her face. Perhaps he preferred wavy hair . . . she wished she'd pinned it up the previous evening.

"It's a wonderful bit of luck, isn't it? It gives us a better chance, doesn't it?"

"You, perhaps."

"You, too. He's a bit of a curmudgeon with everyone, but in his heart of hearts . . ."

"What heart?"

He turned his back on her, took off his lumber-jacket, and put on his white coat.

"I just don't understand you, Vincent," she said softly. "You're a funny person."

"I'm glad someone finds me funny. And now, d'you mind letting me get on with my job?"

His job was to prepare case-histories of new patients who would, in the next few days, be operated on by the Great B or one of his assistants. Vincent was far from patient when he was interviewing, and this was evident from the notes he scribbled over-hastily. He often made spelling mistakes, which Brassart hated. He made a point of humiliating the young man whenever one of them came to his notice. Frequently, there were gaps in the case-histories. "What on earth does this mean, Monsieur Debosse: Past history: none?"

Vincent would then blame the patients. You couldn't get anything out of them. Either they went on and on about imaginary symptoms, omitting to mention the only real symptom which would have led to a diagnosis. Or else the most elementary details had to be dragged out of them, word by word. Their age, for example. There were several who couldn't even remember their date of birth.

On this particular morning there were four new patients, and Vincent feared he wouldn't be through before the Great B was ready. When he arrived, Brassart usually had a private talk with Jean Charbonnier, his favourite assistant, who was known to the others as a pious sneak, but a very good surgeon.

After that, the Great B looked in to see all the patients who had just had an operation. Then came the great event of the day; the group visit to examine the new patients.

As he reached the first floor, Vincent bumped into the duty nurse, Madame Robillot. It was said jokingly that she carried considerable weight in the department—an allusion to her fourteen-stone bulk, nicely distributed. She smiled. Her delicate features were still delightful.

"Monsieur Brassart's here already, Monsieur Debosse."

"I know. He's taken to coming earlier and earlier. Is he ill or something?"

"He's going to operate on Number 22 this morning. Cancer of the oesophagus. What did you have to eat last night?"

This was a familiar question. Since she had become a grandmother, she had taken to trying to mother him. He had once made the mistake of telling her that outside the hospital he lived on bread and cocoa, and the next day she had brought him a bowl of beef stew. Since then he had had to invent complicated menus to forestall her efforts to ensure that he was properly fed.

"Salami, a steak, cheese and red wine," he said quickly. "Excuse me, I must see the new patients."

As he hurried off he heard her calling him a fibber. He continued on his way. He had an awkward, ungainly walk, and his head was always hunched between his stooping shoulders as if he was ashamed of his youth and good looks.

Hélène Accard was beside him again as he was about to open the door of Room 18. She grabbed his arm.

"Don't bother about that one, Vincent. Great B's already seen him. He's in 20 now."

"He's on the group visits already?"

"Yes. Hurry up, for Pete's sake, he's in a frightful temper. He's doing the cancer operation at nine-thirty and he wants to see all the new patients first. Just to make life more difficult for us, I expect."

The door of Room 20 was open and Great B was standing

inside surrounded by his court. He looked like one of the kings in children's history picture-books. His surgeon's cap pulled down severely on his forehead, his chest thrown out, his double chin held high, he was glaring at his acolytes, none of whom showed any inclination to meet his eye. Paying no attention to the patient in the bed, he was listening to Paulet, one of the resident students, who was stammering his observations in an almost inaudible voice. Vincent thought he was saying something about its being an emergency and that the diagnosis wasn't clear-cut.

"It's quite simple," said Brassart, turning finally to the patient. "We have to operate."

The man, who looked about fifty and was very pale, closed his eyes. He whispered that he was in great pain. Brassart patted his hand.

"Three days from now, and you'll be in fine fettle!"

As he turned away from the bedside, he caught sight of Vincent, and turned white. "It's as if I were afraid of this insignificant little student," he thought. "He's making me feel guilty."

He took a grip on himself.

"You don't mind being late, I observe, Monsieur Debosse."

Vincent stammered that he always arrived at this time. "It's just that you've never noticed before, sir." He added that he lived at Asnières, ten miles by road. Brassart advanced on him as if he was going to strike him.

"It makes no difference to me where you live, Debosse. If you had to come fifty miles, you should still be at the hospital by eight-thirty. If you can't get used to conforming to such elementary rules, you'd do better to give up the idea of becoming a surgeon here and now. You're probably better equipped to be a film star, young man!"

Vincent, thinking about the *Internat* examination, tried to smile. He had the effrontery to smile. Brassart thrust his big face forward, as if he had suddenly become very short-sighted. He was obviously on edge, and his dislike seemed so evident that Vincent instinctively recoiled. However, Great B simply burst out laughing, and, followed by his subjects, continued his royal progression back to his office. Vincent, bringing up the rear, felt near to despair. "It's all over with me. I was a fool ever to think the swine would help me."

He had, in the past, been naïve enough to imagine that because he was poor and ambitious, he would remind Brassart of his own youth. But if there was one thing that Brassart did not wish to remember it was his own early poverty, or his desperate and unscrupulous struggle up the first rungs of the ladder of his career.

In his office, Brassart remained standing, his surgeon's cap pushed back now. He surveyed his students with a somewhat absent gaze. He was thinking of Danielle, and felt a curious, sick sensation in his stomach. He had telephoned her probably fifty times during the past ten days, but he might as well have been 'phoning a deaf-mute. When she recognized his voice, she replaced the receiver. The previous evening he had tried to force her door. She had threatened to call the police. The bitch!

He lit a cigarette from a crumpled packet, noticed that his little troop was waiting silently, and smiled.

"Who is to operate on 20?"

"I am, sir," answered Charbonnier.

"Right. Be careful, though. As you saw, the case is rather obscure. I'm wondering about an appendicular perforation. I know the patient has already had an operation."

"Yes, sir. Thirty years ago."

"Thirty years ago, Charbonnier, when you were hardly born, a lot of jokers who thought they were excellent surgeons were opening up bellies left, right and centre. Sometimes they didn't even find the appendix, but they stitched up everything very neatly and the patient was delighted. The morning after he felt fine, and the scar healed up very well. It's possible that your patient was operated on by one of those jokers. It's only a chance in ten thousand, I know, but you shouldn't ignore the possibility. In this case, the patient's own doctor obviously wouldn't have considered appendicitis."

Brassart looked in Vincent Debosse's direction and saw that he was chatting to the Accard girl as if he, the Great B, didn't even exist.

"Debosse!"

His voice exploded like a thunderclap. Vincent started, and then came forward cautiously.

"Perhaps you know so much, Debosse, that you feel I'm wasting your time? Or is it that you have to be treated like an inattentive fourth-former?"

"I'm not sure I understand, sir," said Vincent. He certainly didn't understand. "Why in heaven's name has he got it in for me like this?" he wondered. He gritted his teeth. He felt exhausted. He'd slept badly. He wanted to burst into tears.

"I should be surprised if you did understand, Debosse."

Brassart felt his anger growing. Was he, every time he saw this young man's idiotic face, to feel this unbearable anguish in which all his fears and anxieties were confused? Danielle, his wife, growing old, dying, unfulfilled ambitions. How dare this mediocre young student stare back at him! The young Adonis looked pretty sickly this morning—bags under his eyes, his cheeks hollow, pale.

"Perhaps you've been overdoing it, Debosse. I don't think you're likely to last the course."

"I've been studying sixteen hours a day, sir, for the *Internat*."

"Oh, that's what it is, is it! I had the impression that it was something else. Speaking man to man, Debosse, I think you've been having too many women."

The resident students sniggered. The non-residents were too terrified to draw breath. Hélène Accard, her features tense, was beginning to think Brassart had taken leave of his senses. She was used to his doubtful jokes, his sarcasm and his fits of bad temper, but this was something different. There must be something behind his onslaught upon Vincent.

"No, sir," said Vincent quietly. "I don't have women. I can't afford it."

This time everyone laughed nervously. Brassart lit another

cigarette from the butt of the one he had just finished. He offered the packet to Debosse.

"No, thank you, sir. I don't smoke in the morning."

"Can't afford that, either, I suppose?"

Vincent said nothing. But he wanted to cry out, to hurl abuse. He continued to gaze steadily at Brassart who was rocking his considerable body backwards and forwards, his legs apart, planted firmly on his size eleven feet.

"So you're living in poverty, are you, Debosse! An up-to-date model of the dedicated young man who's willing to starve to death in order to follow a fine, worthy and honourable career."

"That's it, roughly, sir."

Brassart made a royal gesture. His arm described a large circle before coming to rest heavily on Vincent's shoulder.

"Gentlemen, I ask you to look at this remarkable young man who is ready to starve to death to become a surgeon."

Then, without transition, he said: "Tell me, Debosse, are you a mythomaniac?"

"No, sir."

"Then why talk such rubbish? There's no need to starve to death today if you're young and have two arms, two legs and a pretty face."

Vincent's pretty face turned scarlet. "I'll have to throttle him. I'll have to kill him. Whatever it costs me . . ." But at this moment the ward-sister came in.

"Number 22 is ready, sir."

"Right," said Brassart, turning away almost regretfully. He was already in the corridor when he turned abruptly and retraced his steps.

"Come along, Debosse. I want you to be present at this operation."

"But, sir, I've had nothing to do with 22. It's Mademoiselle Accard who should . . ."

"Mademoiselle Accard can deal with the new patients. Are you intending to disobey me, Debosse?"

"No, sir," said Vincent, near to tears.

"God, whatever has got into him?" Vincent asked himself.

"His back, even his back is hateful," he thought as he followed Brassart to the operating theatre. He was dreading the appalling hours to come. He would have been half-witted if he hadn't realized that Brassart intended to use this opportunity to torment him for the rest of the day. Even an operation as lengthy and delicate as that for cancer of the oesophagus couldn't stop Brassart's sarcasms, his obscenities or his dirty jokes. Could anything stop him talking, Vincent wondered. The Great B was most himself in the operating theatre . . . a swine. But a swine who was also a great surgeon.

"What are you dreaming about, Debosse?"

"I was wondering what time we'd be through, sir."

Brassart was washing his hands and Vincent was waiting for a basin to become free.

"It's now nine-thirty. We'll take a twenty-minute break for lunch. You'll be free about six o'clock, young man."

"Free to punch your bloody jaw!" the young man thought.

4

For Vincent Debosse it all began one day in February, the day of the *Internat* examination.

Before entering the small, dreary room that served as a waiting-room, he glanced distractedly in the direction of his fellow-students whose expressions seemed simultaneously relieved, smiling and slightly patronizing. It would be their turn the next day, or the day after that. Vincent guessed that when he walked into the amphitheatre they would feel the same little tug at their hearts that he himself had felt watching his predecessors.

He had come to the Necker Hospital for nothing three days running. Each time he had had to endure the same anguish while the names of candidates were drawn by lot. Today, his own name had been drawn. "This is it! Win or lose. I'm going to pass. No, I'm going to die. God, how dry my mouth is!"

All twelve of them were thinking the same thoughts. All their faces were haggard, their complexions ranging from greyish-green to scarlet. Twelve candidates for the *Internat*. Twelve young people in their twenties who, in ten minutes, would be taking the test which would decide their future as doctors.

"Debosse, give us a fag, there's a good chap! Mine are all gone. There's no need to pull faces, old man!"

"You're not still at school, Delorme. And if I had a mirror on me I'd enjoy showing you your face as seen from this side. Not a pretty sight at all! Here, have a cigarette. But I'd go easy if I were you . . . sure it won't make you sick?"

The beadle, a little tubby man with a pink, bald head and a

quiet voice, began to call the candidates: "Number 2, Monsieur Durieux. Number 3, Monsieur Even. Number 4, Monsieur Depierre . . ."

His palms moist and his stomach plummeting, Vincent prayed that his name wouldn't come out last . . . that is, as Number 1.

"Number 5, Monsieur Debosse."

Forty minutes to wait. It was too long, but he realized that in thirty-five minutes he would be telling himself it was too short. He found difficulty in restraining himself from pushing past the beadle and everyone else and getting the hell out of it all.

Number 1 was Delorme. As Vincent had said, he wasn't a pretty sight—indeed, that was now something of a euphemism. He looked quite frightful. "He's going to pass out. He's trembling too much, he'll never make it," thought Vincent.

"Are you coming, Debosse?"

Someone pushed him towards the sanctum where he was to wait his turn. "Don't worry, old man, it'll be worse at the *Adjuvat*.* Come and sit down. All we need is a bottle of Scotch and some crisps." They were almost all putting on an air of bravado. They loosened their ties, complaining about the heat and the stuffy room. It was scarcely large enough for all of them to squeeze in. They began to talk in nervous, high voices.

"Did you see that programme on the telly about our modern hospitals? Pretty good, wasn't it. They ought to have brought a camera crew to the poor old Necker and shown the masses the sort of conditions we work in. Admittedly, it's supposed to be lucky . . ."

The speaker was a ginger-haired youth with a mass of freckles on his face. His remarks about the television programme seemed to have afforded him great pleasure. Brandishing an imaginary camera in his large hands, he panned it across the waiting-room walls, which had once been yellow but were now just incredibly dirty.

"I say, Debosse, Brassart's on the board. You'll come through with flying colours all right."

* *Adjuvat:* the examination following the *Internat.*

Did he have to reply? Ought he to tell them that the Great B was a bastard, and mad, too? That he, Debosse, was no saint but he had never done anyone much harm, and simply couldn't understand what it was the old man had against him. That he wasn't a brilliant chap, but a steady swot, and that the likelihood was that his chances would be spoiled by his own chief. That the old man probably had his own reasons for hating him, but Debosse himself hadn't the faintest idea what they were. Ought he to say that if he wasn't so absolutely worn out, having lost half a stone in a month from sheer overwork and worry, he would probably have wanted to tackle Brassart and have it out with him, man to man. In any case, he reckoned he didn't stand a chance. He'd finish up as a G.P., like most of the rest of them.

He remained silent, making a vague, meaningless gesture with his head.

For several minutes the lavatories adjoining the waiting-room had been in constant use. It was irresistible. One after the other, the candidates rose, trying to walk naturally and avoid stumbling over their neighbour's feet; then once the door was shut behind them they gave a great sigh of relief. A short respite, a glass of cold water—or even several, downed one after another. A glance in the mirror, only to see a poor wretch with burning eyes and hollow cheeks pleading to be forgotten.

Vincent was no exception to the rule. His most worrying symptoms were his dry throat and his thick tongue, and these were not relieved by several glasses of water. Number 3 had just been called. Number 4, the ginger-haired chap who'd talked about the television programme, lurched up against him as he opened the door of the lavatories.

"Mind out!" he gulped. "Let me get in."

His nose pinched, his face a sickly sweating green above his freckles, he leaped towards a wash-basin. Vincent moved aside in the nick of time.

Outside in the waiting-room they tried to kill time and control their panic.

"I'm leaving this evening for Courchevel. I'm going to chuck my books into the cupboard and forget medicine completely for a fortnight. Sun, mountains, ski-ing and birds. I was beginning to forget their existence. I haven't had a single day off for two years."

They all said more or less the same. The big chap who was Number 11 was already the father of two children. He was hoping to enjoy family life for a few days. Number 7, who was sitting for the fourth time, was intending to sleep eight hours a day until he heard whether or not he had passed.

"Monsieur Debosse!"

Vincent didn't move from his seat. He couldn't think what had happened. Number 4 had only just been called, which should have meant that he still had ten minutes' respite.

"Isn't there some mistake?"

"Number 4 has gone. Come along."

"Hell!" thought Vincent. "Either that ginger-haired chap was really ill, or he couldn't answer the questions at all." He stood up, wondering suddenly if this resolute, stiff automaton marching down a narrow corridor and walking smartly into a white-walled room in which there were two tables could possibly be himself. One of the tables was still occupied by Number 3, and the other was vacant. As he picked up the examination paper he noticed that his hand was trembling. The words blurred. Medical question: amoebiasis affecting liver. Surgical question: malignant renal tumours.

Before sitting down he put his answer sheets and his pen on the table and re-read the questions. The beadle was winding a large kitchen alarm-clock. He turned both hands to point to twelve, and set it in front of Vincent. The race against time was beginning. At twelve-twenty the alarm would ring and the die would be cast, or near enough.

"Now for it," said Vincent to himself. His mind had re-mained a complete blank for a mad minute. He didn't like the two questions. Both of them were full of pitfalls, particularly the medical question, but he knew what to write. He forgot Brassart, forgot the extremely dangerous conflict between them—as dangerous, and as unequal, as his battle with the *Internat*. He

33

pushed on quickly, covering the white paper with words at top speed, with the air of a harmless madman.

When Brassart saw Debosse coming into the amphitheatre he realized that since the beginning of the examinations he had not stopped thinking of Danielle. The first three candidates had babbled on as if they were at the point of death. It was unbelievable how nervous these lads were. He hadn't listened to the question on medicine and had given only half his attention to the one on surgery. This was the state he was in after not seeing Danielle for three weeks . . . unable to concentrate on the examinations, unable to consider objectively proceedings that he had always taken very seriously.

Each day he had told himself that this would be the last, that she would give in, that she wouldn't dare, couldn't possibly manage without him. But it was he who couldn't manage without her. It was an appalling sensation. To be deprived of air couldn't have been worse.

Pale but erect, Vincent walked towards the small desk where he was to face the lions. A glass and a carafe of water were to be his sole support during his trial. He sat down. Behind him were the seats where the others must be waiting. Before him, this massive, green-topped table, and the heads of his ten executioners: the Jury. The hand that laid his papers on the desk was almost steady.

"He's written too much," thought Brassart. "He must have got bogged down in detail. He won't have time to finish."

There was an alarm-clock here, too. Ten minutes to play at being a doctor, not a second more.

" *Major complication of amoebiasis, mainly found in tropical climates . . .*"

"I must be dreaming," thought Vincent. "This isn't me speaking, that terrible, monotonous sound no one seems to be listening to can't possibly be my voice."

He looked at them all, except Brassart who was sitting almost opposite him. They all looked bored, except Brassart.

The Great B seemed to be fascinated by Number 5, though

34

he was listening to him with his mind elsewhere, concentrating on what seemed to be an insoluble problem. The thought of not having Danielle suddenly seemed so appalling that it was like a savage blow in the face. He felt himself losing colour.

". . . *triad of the period of the condition: fever, pains, hepato. . . .*"

Debosse. That was how to get her back. And Debosse was sitting in front of him now. The key was in his hand, he had only to open the door. That, for him, was the significance of candidate Number 5, at whom he was looking, but who was avoiding his eyes. Suddenly he smiled.

". . . *Negative signs: no ascites, no hepatic deficiencies . . .*"

His voice had regained its normal timbre. He was addressing himself to the obstetrician, on the left . . . a bald man with spectacles and a cheery expression. "He isn't even listening to me," thought Vincent glancing at the scribbling pad on which the doctor was doodling. His glance swept automatically towards the centre of the desk and his eyes met those of Brassart. The Great B was smiling at him. Vincent shivered.

"*Diagnostic summary. First: interrogation . . .*"

"God! He's making fun of me. Maybe I'm talking a lot of rot. I don't know whether I am or not. I don't know anything any more . . ."

"*Typical case: an elderly, emaciated colonial, yellowish complexion . . .*"

That awful smile was terrifying him. Suddenly his mind went blank, his voice tailed off and died away like a gramophone running down. He glanced wildly at his notes, but in vain: he had written down only headlines. As he looked up he saw that Brassart's face was quite white. His eyes seemed to be pleading with him. Vincent cleared his throat and went on ". . . *slow development, interrupted by sub-acute recrudescence.*" He rushed through the last part. There was only four minutes left for his question on surgery. He gabbled out his answer at top speed, without lifting his head. He spoke without conviction and forgot one essential detail.

As he stood up he thought: "You've had it, Debosse. You'll

35

have to settle for dosing the great unwashed in the suburbs, that's all you're good for . . . unless you can summon up the courage to try again next year."

Picking up his sheets of notes, he noticed that Brassart, who was no longer looking at him, had turned to Gautrelet, the neurologist. He was talking forcefully to him, making large sweeping gestures. "That's how a chap is shot down in flames," he reflected bitterly as he walked away.

Gautrelet, who was chairman of the jury, equal in seniority with Brassart, and who had two candidates he was supporting himself, made no difficulties. He was perfectly willing to be convinced by the Great B. He would support Debosse. In return, Brassart would support his two candidates. That was the system. However, Gautrelet had his doubts about the reactions of the rest of the jury. The Debosse fellow had not been brilliant. Considered impartially, he deserved 18 out of 30, and it would probably be difficult to convince the others that he deserved 25.

Brassart did not argue about the first three candidates. The consensus of opinion was that they deserved half marks, and that was precisely what they got, since no one on the jury had any special interest in them.

"Debosse, Vincent."

Gautrelet, a small, swarthy man, turned towards the five doctors.

"He began excellently, but on treatment his reply was slipshod," said Ranquet, the gastro-enterologist, who had a yellowish complexion. "I suggest 8 for the question on medicine."

"You must be joking," said Brassart.

"These fools are going to make trouble," he thought. "Best to get in first." He smiled: "Admittedly, I'm not a specialist, but it so happens that I listened to the answer given by Debosse to the question on medicine. That's more than Monsieur Giraldon, for instance, could say," he continued, glancing at the obstetrician. "Right, then! Debosse is my pupil—a brilliant young man who was suffering from a bad attack of examination nerves today. It may be that his answer on medicine was not entirely satisfactory to a gastro-enterologist, but however that may be I found his answer on surgery impeccable, and . . ."

"I'd hardly go so far as that," interrupted Argagnan, who had been appointed chief hospital surgeon the previous year, and whom Brassart did not know.

"As I was saying, I found his answer on surgery impeccable," repeated Brassart, ignoring Argagnan. "Debosse was concise, quick, and didn't get bogged down on unnecessary detail. Should we say, then, 14 for surgery and 11 for medicine?"

"That's crazy!" exclaimed Argagnan. "I suggest 9 for the surgery question, and that's being generous."

"And I suggest 7 for the medicine question," said Vaissière, the pneumatologist, who had failed to be appointed *professeur agrégé* and hated the Great B.

Brassart went on smiling, enjoying himself. He wished Danielle could have been there to admire him.

"Debosse made an excellent impression on me," said the chairman, very gently. "I suggest 14 for his surgery question, and, since Brassart assures that us his pupil merits it, I suggest that the doctors should be a little less severe."

"Impossible!" declared Vaissière. "Debosse doesn't deserve more than 7 for medicine."

"And 9 for surgery," insisted Argagnan.

Brassart was no longer smiling. The game had turned into a battle—his battle to win Danielle back. It was a battle he did not intend to lose. He rose to his feet, picked up his notebook and his pen, saw the same expression of outraged astonishment on each of the nine faces turned towards him. "Bunch of fools," he thought. "Lightweights!" He walked slowly towards the door.

"Brassart!"

It was the chairman and his voice was no longer gentle but full of dismay. Brassart turned. "Yes?" He noted without surprise that there was dead silence and an atmosphere of general anxiety. He waited.

"I'm sure that these gentlemen will see your point of view," Gautrelet went on. "I'm sure they will wish to do their utmost to meet you . . . isn't that so, gentlemen?"

His unprepossessing little face moved from right to left. He was smiling ingratiatingly in an effort to sway the bunch of blockheads who were trying to upset his arrangements with Brassart.

Ranquet, the gastro-enterologist, was the first to surrender. He sighed. A long, deep sigh. Ranquet himself had a pupil he wanted to push—he would probably be coming up the next day—and then there was the Great B's father-in-law, a member of the *Académie de Médicine.* . . No, he would be a fool to stand out against Brassart.

Brassart had come back and sat down at the baize-covered desk.

"Very well," he said, "let's make it 24 for Debosse and forget the matter."

"Next," said the chairman promptly. "We've wasted a great deal of time already."

5

A month. She had held out for a whole month. After that she might well, thought Brassart, find the courage never to see him again. He had written to her, a thing he had once sworn he would never do. In his letter he had told her about Vincent Debosse and the way that he had succeeded in helping his "young protégé". He added that when he saw her again— "soon, I hope"—he would tell her his plans for Debosse.

Danielle's reply had been as prompt as it was laconic: "I await further developments." And now he was really suffering. This was so obvious that his wife felt anxious. Was something worrying him at the hospital? One of the patients? Louise Brassart was neither a very complex nor a very stupid woman. She decided that only professional preoccupations could be the cause of her husband's worried expression, his white face and his poor appetite. She had discovered long ago that he cared about nothing but his work, so there was no point in looking further for an explanation.

For some days she had been aware that Guillaume was not himself. After ignoring her for seven years, he now kept looking at her for no good reason—behaviour embarrassing and almost unseemly in a husband who had been so little her lover.

"Is there a smut on my nose, Guillaume?" she asked, trying to make a joke of his new habit, but he didn't laugh. He studied her with an expression of sombre gravity. He became aware again of her appearance: small and slim, with a delicate profile and short, very dark hair, which was often untidy but which she sometimes managed to control with the aid of a hairpiece.

He was aware that she was beautiful, gentle and entirely admirable. He had never been in love with her, but now it seemed that by being attentive to Louise he was making a start as Danielle's accomplice, conspiring with her, taking the first step towards seeing her again.

Two days after the end of the *Internat* examination he telephoned to ask the results. His protégé was one mark short. He had scored very well in the oral examination, but done only moderately in the written part. Debosse had been accepted as a provisional resident medical student at the hospital, but would have to take the examination again the following year. Brassart was furious. It was as if he personally had suffered an injustice.

"You're certain he's one short?" he demanded. "You haven't made a mistake?"

"No, sir."

"Very well. But check again, anyway. Debosse . . . with a D. First name Vincent. Age, twenty-five."

His informant told him the result three times and then, afraid of losing his temper, hung up.

The following morning Brassart was to take a decision to which he was no longer capable of attaching the importance it deserved. Meeting Vincent in one of the hospital corridors, he stopped to speak to him.

"I'm so sorry, my dear fellow. You must have done badly in the written part. That's the only possible explanation. I can't think of any other reason."

Vincent, who had heard it said that the Great B had fought hard for him and who had finally believed this must be so, smiled feebly.

"Thank you very much for all your help, sir. I . . ."

"Not at all, Debosse, not at all. You can thank me later, but at this moment I have a proposition which I'd like to put to you. Come with me to my office."

Vincent allowed himself to be taken by the arm without showing open reluctance. He was wondering whether he did not prefer the Great B's hostility.

"Sit down, Debosse."

Shifting from one foot to the other, Vincent appeared not to have heard. He was surveying his chief's face, visibly thinner, and his small grey eyes, neither friendly nor unfriendly, but cold and calculating. He began to fear the worst again.

"Sit down, for heaven's sake! There! That's right. Have a cigarette."

He held out his packet of *Celtiques*. Vincent refused, adding that he never smoked in the morning. This reminded Guillaume of the idiotic scene with Debosse just before the *Internat* examination, and increased his difficulty in beginning.

"Well, young man . . . I'm afraid I've sometimes bullied you . . ."

"Bullied me, sir?"

Vincent opened his large, clear eyes wider. Brassart noticed his long, dark eyelashes. "Looks like a doll!" thought Brassart, angrily, yearning to punch him on the jaw.

"You know perfectly well what I mean, Debosse."

"I've forgotten the incident, sir."

"Very well. So much the better. Now listen, my dear fellow . . ."

He stubbed out his cigarette, pushed aside the enormous ash-tray which his students had given him at the beginning of the year, sighed, and lit another cigarette. It seemed to be extraordinarily difficult to get through to this young man. "I shall never get used to the fool," he thought.

"Well, Debosse, I've been thinking quite a bit about you these last few days. I must admit that I have a great deal of sympathy for you, knowing your circumstances. I had a rough time of it myself when I was young. At your age, I was in a financial situation little better than your own, except that . . ."

He was speaking rapidly, his gaze directed above Vincent's head. He hardly dared to meet those doll-like eyes.

". . . So I'm in a good position to understand your difficulties, and I must say that trying to manage on 250 francs a month nowadays . . . Your parents are no longer alive?"

"My mother died last year, sir. I never saw my father. I don't know who he was."

Brassart restrained one of his coarse laughs. "A bastard . . . that's the last straw. This is becoming a real novelette."

"Right. Now listen, Debosse. I should like to help you. Don't ask me why . . . I don't really know myself. And there's no need to give me an answer right away. Take your time and think over my suggestion. What I'm proposing is that you should come to live at my home. We have a large flat, ten rooms, three servants. My two sons are away at boarding-school. My wife would have liked to have five or six children, which is why she chose this flat twenty years ago. She would be delighted to have a young chap like yourself living with us . . . she has found life rather dull since the two boys have been away. The fact of the matter is, my dear boy, that there would be no difficulty at all as far as she is concerned. You would have your own room and your own bathroom, you'd have your meals with us and you'd be able to study in peace and comfort. You must be among the most successful candidates next year, my boy. You'll be absolutely free to work quietly, as and when you wish, in the room that I have in mind for you, which is right at the far end of the flat."

Vincent stared at the floor. His throat felt dry and he thought: "This is a trap, he's making trouble for me, he doesn't give a damn for me or my problems." He wanted to get up, but the naïve expression on Brassart's face deterred him. It seemed both sincere and anxious.

"You've taken me completely by surprise, sir. I simply don't understand. You wouldn't be joking, I suppose . . ."

"Really, Debosse, do you think I'd waste time like that? My proposition is completely serious. I want very much to help you. Think it over. You can give me your answer tomorrow."

He was by now so convinced that this was the only means by which he would succeed in seeing Danielle again that he would willingly have strangled Vincent if the latter had turned his proposal down flat.

"Very well, sir. I'll think it over. You're very kind, and I really don't know how . . ."

He had risen to his feet, his shoulders hunched, his head down, clumsy and embarrassed despite his good looks. He simply didn't believe in this miracle.

"No need for thanks, Debosse. I'll see you tomorrow."

Opening the door and holding out his hand, he repeated:

"Don't forget, then. Tomorrow."

During the first five years of her marriage Louise Brassart had thought she loved her husband, but one day a simple deduction revealed to her that she did not. Guillaume was being unfaithful to her, and yet she felt no jealousy: just mild contempt and a certain annoyance because of the servants.

Louise had always been a very reasonable woman. She had never had the luck to know what love was, but she didn't intend to make a great fuss or have a nervous breakdown because of that. Life offered other pleasures in compensation: fine, intelligent children who would follow in the footsteps of their father and grandfather; the joy of riding in Neuilly or in Chantilly where she had an old house her father had given her; the fun of night life at Cannes with friends in the summer, when she was on her own because Guillaume hated the south of France.

At thirty-eight Louise was not dissatisfied with her body—it was soft and supple like that of a young girl—but she was the only person now to appreciate it. For seven years Guillaume had not knocked at her bedroom door. At least her sleep was undisturbed. But—and this worried her far more—he had, some three months ago, taken to sleeping elsewhere regularly twice a week. This certainly meant that he was having an affair.

For a while Louise had wondered what her husband's mistress was like. She took so much pleasure in imagining this woman that she had not been able to conceal it when she went to confession. The priest had told her to put such dubious thoughts from her mind, however, and she had obeyed. She was a reasonable woman, with a clear, calm mind that had allowed her to recognize the change in Guillaume during the past month.

43

She had worried about it. It was true that he now came home every evening as before, but he spent a great part of the night walking up and down in his bedroom, waking Louise who slept in the room next to his. She felt genuinely sorry for his unhappiness, yet relieved that she had never fallen in love, since, inevitably, love brought suffering.

Moved as she was by his distress, Louise was quite ready to be agreeable to Guillaume, but when he talked to her of bringing Vincent Debosse to live with them she was amazed. Her first impulse was to refuse.

As usual they were dining alone in the large dining-room with its old, dreary furniture. Marie, who had worked for them for twenty years and seemed to be part of the furniture, was serving them. All the same, Guillaume waited until she had left the room to return to the subject:

"Now for heaven's sake don't think it was his idea! Debosse is a very shy, reserved youngster—he wouldn't have dreamed of it. In any case, he may not want to come and live here."

"Why not?"

Louise was wondering what Guillaume really had in mind, for she had never known him to be generous. Probably this young man had rendered him some service.

"He reminds me of my own young days. I never really told you about it, and you never knew, but I had a pretty tough time, you know."

Louise suppressed a smile. She had never told him that she knew all about his past. His parents hadn't been really poor, only nonentities, and it was that above all that he wanted to forget.

"What is Debosse like?"

"Very good-looking," he answered mechanically.

"Very good-looking?"

He saw her amazement and realized that he was behaving like a fool. He had been so clumsy about the whole thing that Louise would end by guessing. But what could she guess? For the time being there was nothing. That fool of a boy, Debosse, would come to live with them, perhaps, and Danielle . . . He sighed, mopped his brow, and looked away to avoid meeting Louise's very dark and very gentle eyes.

"I meant that apart from his great gifts he's not at all unattractive in appearance, as I'm sure you'll agree when you see him."

"Oh."

"He's a very hard-working young man. He'll make a brilliant career for himself if he doesn't have to worry too much about making ends meet."

"So you want him to come and eat and sleep here because he's handsome and so on?"

He shrugged. She's making fun of me, he thought. He swallowed a glass of wine, realizing that he was handling things badly. Louise was in control of the conversation now.

"Oh, well, as you don't like the idea we'll say no more about it."

"But we *must* say more about it, Guillaume."

She was standing up, slim, elegant, composed. She was sure now that he was up to something and that she had been right to suspect his generosity.

"If you think this young man deserves our help I certainly don't want to raise any objection."

A smile hovered on Guillaume's lips.

"Well, I don't want to rush you into anything. Think about it, just think it over," he said gently.

"I've thought about it already. When were you thinking he should come?"

"Whenever suits you."

He was looking very foolish and she was highly amused. He took her by the elbows and stared down at her for a while.

"You're wonderful," he said at last.

"No, Guillaume, just curious!"

Before she went to her bedroom she added: "He'd better come as quickly as possible."

That was the evening when, for Louise Brassart, it all began.

6

He had to go down a long corridor, turn first left, then right, and there was his room, right at the far end. It opened on to a quiet, pleasant courtyard. It was like the room of any young man of good family who was studying endlessly for examinations: that is, not at all practical. He had been obliged to stow a large number of his books in the wardrobe. The small Louis XVI desk was covered with delicate little knick-knacks and he would have to put them away somewhere also—in the bathroom, perhaps. That is, if he remained in this house, which seemed highly unlikely.

He considered the situation, sitting on the edge of a chair like a shy guest, his back straight. When he had told Hélène Accard the previous evening she had advised him urgently not to accept the Great B's offer. "Don't go, Vincent, it's a trap. He hates you, it couldn't be more obvious. Find any old excuse, but don't go."

In fact he could think only of excellent reasons for accepting the invitation. He would be able to study for the exam, eat normal meals, and buy himself a new suit, and he wouldn't have to bother any more about his own domestic problems. It was an astonishing but very tempting thought. In the end he had said "yes" in a shaky voice, feeling reasonably sure that if he had said "no" he would have regretted it always.

"And here I am," he thought, biting his nails. "The young man's story begins a new chapter." He had just met Madame Brassart, and their conversation could scarcely have been

shorter. "I don't know how to thank you, Madame . . ."
"Not at all. . . ." She had not given him the impression of
being at all stuck-up, but she seemed remote, patrician, pretty
perhaps—"I hardly looked at her face." It was Brassart who
had accompanied him to his room. "Make yourself at home,
Debosse, and if there's anything you want, call Marie—she can
fix it. She'll let you know when dinner is ready."

He was dreading above all this first meal with the Brassarts.
He would have to talk, to tell them about himself, to explain . . .
But what could he explain? That the Great B had gone off his
head? That after loathing and humiliating him he was now
doing something for him which he had probably never done for
anyone else?

He stood up and went over to the window looking out on the
courtyard. Everything was quiet and peaceful, the whole room
was inviting him to feel happy, but he was seized with appalling
anxiety. He felt a lump of ice in his chest, his heart was thump-
ing, and his palms were damp and sweaty as he rubbed his eyes.
"Not a second to lose! I must chuck my things into my bag and
go. I'll never ever see the Great B again."

However, he didn't budge. Leaning against the window,
dreaming of a courage that he lacked, he let time pass, sweeping
away his impulses, calming his anxiety, bringing him craven
resignation. When Marie knocked at his door, he started, and
shouted, "Just coming" before she had even spoken. He felt
a complete fool and regretted he had not had the courage to
leave. Now there was no choice but to enter the lion's den.

Madame Brassart was wearing an enchanting dark-green
dress in a fine, shiny wool which Vincent thought must be silk.
He would have liked to be able to forget his own old, badly cut
suit, which he had worn every day for three years and which he
had had pressed that morning without much success. Seated
on Madame Brassart's right, he was facing the Great B, who was
staring at him with bored attention. He looked down at the
tablecloth, his ears reddening, his hands on his thighs. There
was so much cutlery on the table that he was afraid of using the
wrong things. He was, in fact, afraid of everything—of Marie's

extreme politeness and of Madame Brassart's indulgent smile. Trying to eat delicately, he stared at the wall on his right where hung an appropriately melancholy painting by Boudin.

Brassart was speaking. His rough voice sounded gentler, better modulated than usual . . . perhaps because his wife was there. He was talking of people and things unknown to Vincent, and Madame Brassart seemed to be listening with her mind elsewhere. From time to time she murmured "yes, of course," or "no, I didn't know" in a monotonous, expressionless tone which must surely exasperate even the most easygoing of men eventually.

She interrupted her husband to ask Vincent if he liked his room. If he needed anything he mustn't hesitate—Marie would look after it. The conversation died and was followed by a heavy silence. Vincent thought he ought to say something, no matter what, no matter how idiotic. He had scarcely opened his mouth, and that was only to say "yes" to everything. Whatever would she think of him? He found the courage to turn his head towards her, and met her very dark eyes looking intently at him; and they were not averted when they encountered his glance. "She's looking me over like a new piece of furniture, carefully, without embarrassment. That's what I am to her . . . a piece of furniture."

Louise was thinking that she'd never seen anyone like this young man. A wonderful face! But why the tragic, faintly absurd air about him?

"A little more?"

"No, thank you, Madame Brassart. I'm not very hungry today."

"You must eat," Brassart interrupted. "When I was a lad I ate like a horse."

Vincent said he wasn't exactly a lad any more . . . twenty-five.

"And at twenty-five, sir, you were already in your third year of the *Internat*."

Brassart mumbled that he had just been lucky. Before gulping down what was left on his plate he glanced quickly at

48

his watch. In less than an hour he would be with Danielle, she was expecting him. Her voice on the telephone had sounded exactly as he remembered it: low, quiet, a little husky. "I'd like to see you, Guillaume. Come round quickly." Although he had told her that Debosse was now living in his house, she had made no comment, but he was not foolish enough to think she would not mention the matter again. She would work round to the subject with the wary expression she wore when she had money troubles. He would be ready. He was playing her game, wasn't he? But in fact there would be another game he was playing: his own. He caught himself smiling, and, lifting his head, found two pairs of eyes watching him. He had forgotten them.

"Will you be working this evening, Debosse?" he asked hastily.

"I work every evening, sir."

"That's fine."

Louise realized that she was to be left on her own. Whatever problem had been troubling Guillaume had, apparently, been settled now. She wondered how far Debosse had been responsible for this.

She rose to her feet and the two men followed suit. Vincent was wondering if he could say goodnight immediately or if good manners demanded that he should stay and talk for a while.

"Well, we mustn't keep you, Debosse. If you feel like working now, seize the opportunity. Goodnight."

Brassart held out his hand, and Vincent put his own damp, delicate hand in it. "Goodnight, sir," he said. Then he turned to Madame Brassart who was looking at him again as if he was a piece of furniture—or so he thought. He hoped foolishly for a smile or a kind word, but Madame Brassart's "goodnight" was as perfunctory as that of her husband. Vincent vanished, rather than left the room.

Louise was meditating. She gazed at her husband's boxer profile. He was lost in a reverie in which she played no part.

"Are you going out this evening?"

49

"An important meeting," he said, failing to keep his voice quite steady.

"Ah, well . . . goodnight, then, Guillaume."

She was smiling, charming, natural. Reassured, he smiled back.

"I suppose you'll be watching your television?"

"Probably."

She had had the set put in her room because Guillaume couldn't bear "all that rubbish". She watched almost every evening, alone, sedate. She watched everything, nothing was too trashy for her. She didn't dislike trash, it didn't offend her; indeed it reassured her somehow.

Just as she was about to switch on the set, she changed her mind without knowing quite why. She ran her bath, dropped in some bath salts, removed her make-up carefully, and then took off her dress, her lace brassière and her nylon slip, and let herself slide into the warm, foamy water like the young, doe-eyed starlet in a film she had once seen.

She stroked her shoulders gently, smoothed the foam over her small, rounded, vulnerable breasts. Suddenly she felt terribly sad.

Danielle was waiting for Guillaume. She had been waiting for more than a month, her moods oscillating between rage, panic and wild hope. Today, however, she felt lucid, intelligent and courageous. She felt she had earned her luck. Luck? She pressed the palm of one hand on the oak table and kept it there for several seconds without moving.

He was ringing the bell. Two short rings. She hunted hastily for her mirror. Was her make-up too heavy? A bit, yes. "I'm looking older." She opened the door and he came in. "He's here! He's mine. Almost!"

He seized her in his big arms and gave her a smile of genuine delight. She was wearing a silk dressing-gown, and was naked beneath it. Her flesh was soft, white and scented. He was with her again. It all seemed so simple now. As she moved away to pour him a whisky her dressing-gown fell open, revealing her rounded breasts and her flat belly. She retied the belt, blushing like a schoolgirl. She seemed nervous and ill at ease, but he found no difficulty in adapting himself again to the situation. He threw his overcoat on a chair, walked round the room, rediscovered the same awful furniture, the same pink and blue walls, and the same slightly cloying smell—a mixture of expensive scent, toilet preparations and English cigarettes. As he sat down on the settee he told her that he was feeling fine now, that he had plenty of time, that he would stay the night if she would like him to do that.

"This is your home . . . with me."

She was thinking about Louise. How would she take it? And Debosse? Suddenly she wondered if the boy was really as submissive and as naïve as Guillaume claimed.

"I'm ready to listen now. Tell me everything."

She was sitting beside him, pulling her dressing-gown over her pretty knees and looking at him composedly with that deceptive air of innocence which had attracted him to her that first day at Orly airport.

"There isn't very much to tell. Debosse is settled in with me. And I'm here. And I love you."

"I love you, too," she said, her thoughts elsewhere. She was thinking of any number of more important things than love. What good was love to a woman ravaged by fear of loneliness, by fear of the future? But he didn't seem to understand. He was there, as he said, settling back into his little ways.

"Well?" she asked.

"Well, it's a question of waiting."

She pushed his hand away.

"Waiting for what?" she demanded.

He took a deep breath. She was rushing him and the vague phrases he had prepared seemed ridiculous now.

"Waiting for what?" she asked again.

"Oh, I don't know. . . Are you working again?"

"I'm doing temporary secretarial jobs."

"You've deserted Orly?"

"Orly deserted me. What are you intending to do about your wife?"

"Nothing much at the moment. Kiss me!"

She kissed him as he asked, but it was the only concession he would get as long as he refused to talk about the Debosse business. She had been waiting a long time and imagining this evening with Guillaume, with everything going her way, not his, at last. She had vowed that never again would she allow herself to be fobbed off with vague promises that he never intended to keep. Things had to be cut and dried now, right from the start, even if it meant a showdown. Only then would she reassume her role of the pretty redhead with whom men had always been pleased to sleep, the pretty redhead who could be picked up and dropped, who was required only to be pretty and a redhead. Except that this time her man wasn't going to get away.

"What are you intending to do about your wife?"

"Oh, for God's sake! You're in such a hurry it's indecent. Besides, you'd do better to be more subtle. I wasn't expecting to be greeted like this."

He wasn't smiling now. His hopes had been disappointed, and he loathed the little tug at his heart which made him feel breathless.

She said that this wasn't what she had been expecting, either. She had been expecting him to come with precise details of his plans. He wondered what details he was going to have to invent from now on if Danielle continued to prove so intractable.

"You can't expect something like this to work out in a day. You must grasp that."

She had risen to her feet, hating him, seeing him for exactly what he was. He was ready to promise anything while he thought he was likely to lose her, but as soon as she gave in to him he'd prove as untrustworthy as any other man. But this time she wasn't going to give in to him.

"I've grasped that it could all be settled in a few minutes if you really wanted it, and if Debosse is as stupid as you say."

He looked into her green, iridescent, disturbing eyes.

"What do you mean?"

52

She replied that he knew perfectly well what she meant, or if he didn't by now the whole thing was hopeless.

Louise's death. The first time he'd talked about it he had launched out into a story so fantastic that he had never dreamed Danielle could take it seriously. But, in any case, that had been no more than talk. Anyone can talk. To say something like that you needed simply to be a fool who was no longer very young, no longer very attractive, and to have suddenly discovered that a woman could drive you out of your mind with her soft skin, and her way of sitting and closing her eyes. A fool like that might say any outrageous nonsense. He had talked like a fool and gone on to plot like a gangster. And he was the Great B!

"But after all," he thought, in an attempt to reassure himself, "what man—after twenty years of marriage—hasn't thought of the possibility of murdering his wife and getting away with it?" It was simply that he had thought out loud, that was the only difference. But out loud in front of Danielle . . . that had been his first mistake. He remembered his own words: "If I got young Debosse living with us, Louise would fall in love with him—or he with her, which would be much better. In any case, the servants would be sure that Debosse was involved in some way with my wife. When everything was set, I'd intervene, very calmly, and tell Louise that I was giving Debosse one week to clear out and find himself somewhere else to live. Then, just before his departure, my wife would be murdered one evening when she was known to have been alone in the flat with him. I'd be able to make sure afterwards that he couldn't prove his innocence."

Madness! Only a lunatic could have believed such nonsense. Only a lunatic could have talked like that. But he *had* talked like that. He flushed and felt his face turning red from the roots of his hair to his neck.

"You're mad!"

"I haven't said anything."

He stood up and began walking slowly up and down. Two more steps and I go. Two more steps and I take her in my arms and force her to forget all about this idiotic idea. Two more steps . . . I'll try to gain time. He went up to her and took her by the shoulders.

"Look! This is all I'm suggesting, the only practical possibility: that Debosse, who is now living in my flat, falls in love with my wife, becomes her lover, and I sue for divorce. Louise couldn't refuse."

She was laughing. Loudly, but mirthlessly. He shook her.

"Stop it, for God's sake!"

"Your wife!" she exclaimed. "Do you really imagine that an attractive young man like Debosse with all the girls falling over themselves to have an affair with him would dream of making love to your dreary, pious old wife?"

"Debosse is a climber. Even if he doesn't find my wife attractive, he'll try, if only to be sure of living permanently with us."

He was wondering why he bothered to talk to her about this plan, even though it was less crazy than the other. What he should do was to get out double-quick, end the whole silly business, pick up the first girl he saw and forget all about Danielle.

She was saying that precisely because Debosse was a climber he'd never take the risk of sleeping with the wife of his benefactor. Even if he found her attractive, he would presumably have enough self-control not to fall into a trap like that.

His face pale and sagging, Guillaume kept remembering the other plan, the plan that had started all this trouble, the plan he had talked about one day when he had thought he would go out of his mind if he lost this irritating little bitch.

"I never said anything like that, never . . ." he muttered stupidly.

"Anything like what?"

"Nothing."

"Let go of me," she said.

"No. What were you hoping? Come on, out with it."

"Have you forgotten you promised to marry me?"

He let go of her, picked up his overcoat, and stood in front of her, thinking: "If I go now, shall I have the courage not to 'phone her, not to plead with her?" He remembered the hateful month he had just lived through, missing her, needing her as he needed oxygen. He slumped into an armchair.

"It's completely ridiculous," he said. "Anyway, Debosse isn't a fool or a madman. You mustn't underestimate him. And the risks . . . the risks would be enormous."

She looked at him in surprise and with new hope.

"Who would have any hesitation in accepting the word of a great man like yourself against that of an insignificant little student who'd been dragged up out of the gutter? It's as simple as that."

It was too awful. He stood up, almost unrecognizable. Suddenly he was himself again, the Great B, with his impressive face, his bold glance, his square shoulders. He began pulling on his overcoat, thinking: "She really is mad, she's capable of anything. But who could she find to do such a thing?" Danielle realized that she had lost the first round.

"Are you going?"

He didn't answer, but opened the door. She called his name, clinging to his arm and crying. Real tears. He let her drag him to the settee and sat down like a sleep-walker, his mind a blank. She was saying that she loved him, begging him to forget the "misunderstanding", telling him that he hadn't understood. All she wanted . . . all she wanted at this moment was that he should stay with her, and that they should be at peace together. Had he stopped loving her? Didn't he want her any more?

Later—much later—when all the lights were out, she said suddenly: "How will he set about seducing your wife?"

Guillaume had closed his eyes. He was floating on the edge of sleep where everything becomes a little blurred.

"What? What are you talking about?"

"I'm talking about Vincent Debosse . . ."

Without giving him a chance to reply, she went on: "Because there's not much time to lose, Guillaume. I'm going to have a baby."

55

7

Not until ten days after his arrival at the Place Malesherbes did Vincent have occasion to dine alone with Louise. He didn't know if he should feel pleased at the prospect. It couldn't be worse than having to suffer Brassart's presence. The Great B's silences, and the eccentricities of his behaviour, had been terrorizing Vincent. Each day he resolved to leave this household, but the thought of his examination continued to make him hesitate. As for Louise . . . she was just a woman like any other, no less boring, no more worthy of his attention.

Glancing at her that evening, however, as she entered the dining-room, he thought she had changed. She seemed much more relaxed. Her make-up was also more skilfully applied and her hair more becomingly arranged—not that Vincent was aware of details of this sort. He felt wretched, and hunted, and his expression was as hang-dog as usual. Louise found it impossible to cajole a smile out of him and the conversation remained limited to conventional and formal exchanges. For Louise, who had been looking forward to this meal alone with him, this was more than a disappointment—it was a failure.

"Are you worried about something, Vincent?"

He felt himself blush. It was the first time she had addressed him by his first name. He said that everything was fine, thank you . . . fine. Except that . . .

"Except that. . . ?"

Marie had come into the room to clear the soup plates away. He glanced at Louise and thought her both beautiful and touching, but for someone other than himself. He had never allowed himself to waste time on women. He had had a few easy, brief adventures. All—or almost all—women were easy. Those were his only memories of women.

Marie was holding a dish in front of him. As he served himself he let a small piece of fish fall on the tablecloth. He stifled an exclamation of dismay and tried to repair the damage, making matters worse. Louise laughed.

"Leave it, leave it!"

Then, realizing that the incident had infuriated him, she added:

"It's funny, all you surgeons are so clumsy outside the operating theatre. When Guillaume tries to mend something at our country house it's always a disaster."

His head bent, his annoyance scarcely abated, Vincent had the feeling that she was waving indulgence at him like a flag, that she was as polite and insincere as all women in her sort of world. "And what am I expected to do next?" he thought angrily. "Go down on my knees?" He scowled. Marie left the room and Louise put her hand on his. "I wish you'd tell me what's wrong," she said.

He muttered "nothing . . . nothing at all," bent low over his plate, and began to eat very quickly and very ungracefully, as he had learned to do at Asnières.

Louise watched him with a baffled expression. For three days she had thought of him constantly. This neither surprised nor dismayed her, that was how it was, and she wasn't going to draw absurd conclusions from the fact. This handsome young man had been offered to her, and she was welcoming the gift with all the passion of which she alone knew herself to be capable. That was all.

"You aren't happy here, Vincent. What is it you don't like?"

Her voice was quiet, gentle, and devoid of mockery.

"Everything," he said. As he looked up his eyes met hers . . . surprised and hurt. "I suppose I'm behaving badly, but you asked me. I've told you the truth, that's all."

She tried to smile. He waited until she had stood up before rising himself.

"Well, I must get on with my work," he said awkwardly.

"Are you going to leave us, Vincent?"

She had taken him by the hand and her own was burning.

"I think you're a bit feverish, Madame Brassart," he said coldly. "You ought to go to bed early."

"Are you going to leave us?"

"I don't know."

He stayed. He found good arguments for staying, and they were always the same: his exam, Brassart's influence, the new suit he hadn't yet bought. He even tried to work very hard. He also did his best to avoid Louise, always finding some pretext for cutting short their time together when the Great B was dining out.

He did not, however, feel really calm, except during the week-ends, which the Brassarts spent at Chantilly. At such times the flat in the Place Malesherbes was entirely his own. He took his meals in the kitchen, slopped around in pyjamas, made a tour of inspection of all the rooms. One Sunday, when he had gone into Louise's room to watch the television, he couldn't resist the temptation to rummage about. He opened the wardrobe where all her clothes were hanging neatly. Her perfume still lingered on them. He stroked the materials and lifted out a dress, a yellow dress with a smooth, easy swing from the waist. He thought of his mother and her eternal little black dresses in cheap material, he thought of the women who had said they loved him, and of the ones who had bored him to death, and he thought of all the stupid things he had done.

In a Louis XV chest-of-drawers he found an old photograph album. There was the Great B, young and very thin, on his wedding day; and Louise, quite lovely in a long, white dress. Really lovely. A few pages on, two adolescent faces, serious and delightful—the Brassart children. Vincent had seen them once at the Place Malesherbes. Two lanky, noisy boys whom their mother seemed to adore, but who were

58

brought up very strictly. They were allowed out of school only one Sunday a month, when they usually spent the day at Chantilly with their parents.

It was in this album, slipped between two loose photographs, that he found the letter. It was typed, and addressed to Madame Brassart. He read it: an anonymous letter warning Louise to be on her guard against the young man lodging with her. Vincent was so surprised that he did not at first realize that it referred to himself. When, finally, he could no longer avoid recognizing himself in this portrait of a young social climber, unbalanced and likely to stop at nothing, he laughed . . . but uneasily. He sat still for some minutes, his head in his hands— an ambitious young man, but irresolute.

His periods of calm came to an end the following week when Brassart invited him to spend the week-end at Chantilly.

"The weather's perfect, Debosse. You're beginning to look a bit peaked. It'll do you good to get a breath of fresh air. We'll leave you to your own devices. I catch up on my letters and my reading at the week-ends, and my wife's out riding most of the time."

It was Louise who had insisted on his inviting Vincent.

"As you've taken responsibility for this young man's welfare, you might as well do the thing properly. Ask him to Chantilly for the week-end."

"You must be mad!"

"Why? It seems only reasonable to me."

He said she was carrying things too far.

"Before we know where we are, Debosse will be thinking he's doing me a favour by living under my roof."

She laughed. She felt as if she was twenty again, self-willed and spirited.

"If he bores you so unbearably send him away. You obviously hate the sight of him, but if you keep on moaning about him I shall start trying to find out just why you brought him here in the first place."

She had her way. Guillaume grumbled but invited Debosse

to Chantilly, and Vincent could not do other than accept. Only Louise seemed pleased.

The house at Chantilly came as a surprise to Vincent. He had expected a mansion, but it was an old, rather shabby little house, which wasn't even comfortable. The large rooms were white-painted and furnished in a vaguely rustic style. In each of the bedrooms there was a brass bedstead and a black-and-white tiled floor. Vincent was puzzled. The Brassarts could have afforded a very nice house with every possible comfort, like the ones he had seen in American magazines, yet they chose to live here.

The garden was not in much better shape than the house. The long grass would have shocked even a moderately conscientious gardener. When Louise asked him to come out for a stroll, he could scarcely refuse. After a short walk, during which she explained to him that the house and the garden were the children's domain, and that she and her husband were not allowed to change anything whatever, she asked him to put two deck-chairs in the sunshine.

"You look so pale, Vincent—the sunshine will do you good."

He took off his jacket, loosened his tie and rolled up his shirt-sleeves, but he still felt uncomfortably warm. The sun was very hot. Louise was looking at him . . . she never seemed to tire of looking at him. He decided he would just have to get used to it.

He was bored. No matter how far back he searched his memory, he couldn't remember ever having idled, but he didn't have the imagination to think of an excuse to escape.

"Aren't you going riding this afternoon?"

She said she felt rather tired.

"I'd better leave you then."

He had stood up as he spoke, but she caught his hand.

"No, please stay."

There was such tenderness in her voice that he felt rather foolish. He sat down again and lolled back, his arm behind his head. He closed his eyes against the glare of the sun, and also to avoid Louise's steady stare.

After a few minutes he dropped off to sleep, waking ten minutes later with a startled cry. She was bending over him and her hand—a very pretty hand—was touching his neck. It was almost a caress. He pushed it away brusquely.

"What's the matter?" he demanded.

"Nothing, nothing at all."

She was looking down at him with great tenderness.

"What were you doing?"

"You were perspiring. Your face looked very flushed, as if you were choking. I thought I ought to loosen your tie."

"I'd loosened it already."

"Not enough."

She was smiling, but he felt angry. He stood up and she moved closer to him, her face very near his, her body almost touching his. It was he who said: "I think I'd better go."

He realized he was behaving boorishly, and also that he was afraid. She didn't move. He stepped aside, picked up his jacket, laid it over his arm, and then, without looking at her, he said:

"Do you know what you're doing?"

She didn't reply, but as he began to walk towards the house he thought he heard her murmur that she loved him.

"Perhaps I'm falling in love with her, too. I'm getting to be crazy enough for anything. They've contaminated me, they're making me as nasty as they are themselves."

He had just gone up to his bedroom after a very difficult evening. During dinner Brassart had poked fun continuously at his scarlet, sunburned cheeks and nose; and despite the presence of his wife he had been telling some of his most vulgar jokes.

"And every time I look up there she is staring at me. Is she an hysteric? She can't be, she's too lucid, too self-controlled."

His head on his arms on the table, he tried to think things out.

"I suppose it's quite obvious, really. The Great B invited me here to become his wife's lover, and now that I'm engaged on these unpleasant speculations, why shouldn't I admit that she's probably his accomplice? That she entered willingly into a plan to seduce me? But why? Why me? What's their game?"

He stood up, breathing heavily. His throat felt constricted and his hands were icy.

"I've always been poor, but healthy. Now I have my first experience of the good life and I become neurotic. Treatment?"

He managed to pull himself together and tried to settle to his work. He was reading a medical journal when the door of his room opened gently. Turning his head, he saw her. She was wearing black slacks and a white blouse. She stood in the doorway, her arms at her sides, shy, charming.

"Is there anything you need, Vincent?"

He stood up, but remained where he was.

"Please don't come in, Madame Brassart."

"There's no need to be frightened."

He felt she was treating him like a child, with great patience, indulgence, and something else. He wanted none of this something else. He would resist it with all his will-power.

She closed the door and leaned back against it.

"As you've probably noticed, the service here isn't very good. Marthe, our old cook, has to do everything. She may have forgotten something you need."

"She hasn't forgotten anything, thank you."

"You are working?"

It seemed that nothing was going to get rid of her. He wanted to say that yes, he was working, yes, she was disturbing him, yes, he had had enough of her glances, her silly virgin sighs, her old maid's dreams.

"No," he heard himself saying. "I wasn't really working. I was thinking about you."

She took a step towards him.

"Don't!" he exclaimed sharply.

She obeyed, but continued gazing at him intently. Her admiration was so frank that he blushed beneath his sunburn. He stammered that there must be some misunderstanding, that he wasn't like other chaps of his generation, at least, not

62

like those written about so much in the press and in novels. But he wasn't all that unusual, either. It was just that he didn't enjoy playing around with women. It just didn't interest him, that was all. He had better things to do.

As she went on standing there, her arms at her sides, gazing at him, and as he could hardly push her out of the room, he began talking about himself.

"I'm at a great disadvantage, don't you see?"

No, she didn't see.

"Well, the way I grew up."

He told her about Asnières, his childhood at the back of the delicatessen shop where his mother worked. Squalid years. Not unbearable . . . just squalid.

"Do you know what I mean?"

Louise assented with a nod of her head, but she couldn't really see why this handsome young man was dwelling so vehemently on his wretched past. When he fell silent she said nothing to encourage him to speak again. The silence made Vincent feel more vulnerable than ever. He became more aware of her, almost moved by her, but the sound of a door opening on the floor above gave him an excuse to suggest that it would be better if she went back to her own room.

He slept very little that night.

"I may not be like other chaps of my generation, but I'm a man, after all."

He felt resentful towards her, he would have liked never to see her again. However, when he went downstairs the next morning he was disappointed to find that she was already out riding.

At breakfast, Brassart announced that they would be leaving for Paris at three o'clock. He wanted to avoid the traffic jams and to arrive in good time. He had an important engagement.

"In any case, I'll say it once and for all, my dear Louise, this place bores me stiff."

The important engagement was with Danielle. She was not expecting him, but he was going to call on her nevertheless. He needed to see her all the more because Louise was aggravating his bad temper. Making sheep's eyes at young Debosse and not caring who noticed. It was intolerable.

But Danielle's behaviour was just as irritating. No scenes, no quarrels, but a suspicious calm. She didn't speak of Louise or of Debosse. At Guillaume's suggestion she had given up her temporary typing jobs. The work was altogether too wearing for such miserable wages, he had told her. Money need never be a problem between them. And then, as she was pregnant . . . Yes, she would have the child. Yes, she would have it looked after by an excellent foster-mother. Yes, she would wait till things were better. Yes, she felt fine. No, it was not a question of indifference, but of becoming resigned to her situation. Guillaume felt that he didn't understand the woman he loved.

In fact, Danielle was playing her last card and this time she intended it to be an ace. She remarked that she had received a new offer from Nice, and the climate and the working conditions appealed to her. She pretended that she was on the point of accepting the job. She was bluffing.

He protested vehemently.

"Then why don't you let me work for you? I'm bored doing nothing, and you're always grumbling about your secretary. I'd be much better than she is."

She had guessed he would begin by refusing, but she thought that he would soon change his mind. Very soon he would be ready to give in over anything.

She had become convinced of this as soon as he had come in that particular Sunday. His eyes were angry and his expression humourless.

"We've won!" he declared, sounding rather like a boxer who has been beaten. "My wife is in love with Debosse."

"And what about him?"

"He's floundering. He's like a mouse sniffing at a piece of cheese. Shall I, shan't I?"

"He will," she said. "But perhaps he'll need a push."

She had grown plumper than she had been when he first met her. She was wearing a simple, plain linen dress and had given up the dark make-up which made her look older. He thought she looked very lovely. As he took her in his arms he told her he had thought things over and could see no reason why she shouldn't work as his secretary. Louise wouldn't even notice that she was pretty. Louise had eyes for no one except Debosse. She could begin work the next day.

His former secretary had been dismissed, with three months' pay, on the pretext that she wasn't prepared to work at Chantilly more than one week-end in four. She wept. The one Sunday a month she sacrificed already was quite a lot, wasn't it? Would Monsieur Brassart be able to find anyone sufficiently devoted, or sufficiently stupid, to sacrifice all her Sundays?

"Yes," said Guillaume briskly. "It's all fixed up. But I quite appreciate your reasons for refusing."

He also made her a present of a thousand francs.

Danielle came to the Place Malesherbes. For once Guillaume was right, for Louise glanced only casually at her husband's new secretary. The meeting with Debosse was more disturbing. Danielle, who had never been able to resist young and handsome men, did her utmost to charm him, but to no avail. He recognized in her the type of woman who had pursued him ever since he was old enough to make love. Her effusive manner put him off and he scarcely bothered to be polite. It was not, however, until some days later that he realized she was Brassart's mistress.

"So that's what it's all about," he thought. "It all depends on me. This is why I'm supposed to become Louise's lover. That's what they're all waiting for."

He felt no inclination to treat this revelation as a joke. Deep misgivings haunted him until gradually he began to feel sure that this was more than a conventional marital "arrangement". He sensed that somehow Louise was in danger, and suddenly he knew that he was really in love with her.

8

The Great B was finding the realization that he was growing old quite unbearable—his distress exceeded the bounds of reason—and the evidence of the extent to which Vincent's youth and good looks had transfigured Louise was driving him out of his mind. A man can be jealous about a woman he doesn't love in a thousand different ways, and Brassart's way was the most deadly and the most stupid.

Those evenings which he didn't devote to Danielle he spent spying on Louise and Vincent. Ostensibly he settled down in his study very early, but he crept out noiselessly later in the hope of surprising them. For several days he was obliged to recognize that nothing was happening, then, one particularly mild evening, he heard footsteps on the terrace. Louise and Vincent.

Vincent had opened the French windows of his room. Opposite him, some few yards away, was Louise. She was standing outside her own bedroom, looking at the young man. He was sure she had waited on this circular verandah evening after evening. Once again, it was she who took the first step. She walked past her husband's bedroom, past her children's bedroom, and on to the part of the terrace facing the dining-room. Garden chairs and a table stayed out there all the year round.

After about ten minutes Vincent, staring down at his feet, sauntered round to join her.

"Good evening, Vincent."

He told himself he would never learn how to talk to her.

"Good evening, Madame Brassart."

They sat down in two of the armchairs, with a table

between them. He laid his slim hands on it, stared at them, and then looked at her. He thought her very beautiful this evening in her light, *décolleté* summer dress.

"That woman," he muttered, "your husband's secretary . . . I can't stand her."

"Why not?"

"Don't you see?"

"She's of no importance."

Now he was the one who couldn't see. He had principles, the moral principles of the poor. Madame Brassart no longer loved her husband—well, that was one thing—but she shouldn't tolerate the presence of her husband's mistress under her own roof. You'd have to be blind not to see how voracious Danielle Fellegrini was. This was more than a passing, commonplace adultery. He wasn't sure yet what the danger was, but he knew it was very real.

He said no more, for fear of seeming indiscreet or ridiculous.

Louise in her turn placed her hands on the table, moving them imperceptibly towards Vincent's. Their fingers touched lightly. Suddenly she turned her head towards the French windows, thinking she had heard something, but there was nothing to be seen. She smiled.

Without switching on the lights, Guillaume had entered the dining-room. He saw their silhouettes outlined against the French windows and hid behind the partly open curtains. He stood watching them, remembering the time when he and Louise were engaged. She had said then that she loved him, but she had never turned to him as she was turning now towards Vincent.

He watched them for a long time. They looked like two gentle, radiant lovers, secure in their happiness. For some weeks now Guillaume had felt in himself a growing desire to kill Vincent.

"Two months ago, I was on the point of leaving Danielle because she had dared to suggest I should kill my wife," he reflected; "yet today I can think calmly about murdering Debosse. A different victim . . . and perhaps I've become a different man."

As he returned to his study he felt completely composed. Taking his revolver—a Mauser he had picked up during the war—from a drawer, he found himself searching his mind for some reasonable justification for his intentions. He had offered Debosse hospitality in his home, and now Debosse was making love to his wife; he had given the young fool a unique opportunity for furthering his career, and this was his gratitude; but Brassart was obliged to admit to himself that these rationalizations were absurd. The fact was that Debosse was irritating him like a tiresome fly. He wanted to be rid of him. He intended to do away with him . . . but he wasn't going to take pointless or careless risks. Before replacing the revolver in the drawer, he checked that it was loaded.

It wasn't until rather later, when he was lying in bed, that he remembered Danielle. If he killed Debosse, the adultery would be proved and divorce would become a mere formality; at least, that would be how Danielle would see it. But what about himself? He turned out the light, rolled on his side and closed his eyes, preferring not to think about that. He would rather not admit to himself that never, never had he really contemplated divorce.

Brassart had bought a tape-recorder. In the evenings he dictated the letters that Danielle typed the next morning while he was with his patients.

In a few days the new secretary had completely captivated Marie and Francine, the cook. Danielle had settled into Brassart's study where she worked all day, then, at five o'clock, Marie brought her a cup of tea and they had a chat. Danielle's slightly faded film-star face fascinated the irredeemably ugly Marie, who had never felt the touch of an exploring male hand, and read the lonely hearts columns regularly between the lunchtime washing-up and preparations for dinner.

Danielle soon knew her way around the flat as well as if she had lived there for years. She rarely met Louise, and when she did she passed her as unobtrusively as possible, but she put herself out to cross Vincent's path as often as possible. She got no more than curt nods and formal greetings for her pains.

"You look like a bear with a sore head!" she said mockingly to him one day.

68

"I'm not a ladies' man."

"It depends on who the lady is, I'd say."

He stopped in his tracks and turned back towards her. She was smiling, beautiful, too heavily made-up, very sure of herself.

"Is there anything I can do for you?" she asked lightly.

"Yes," he said shortly. "Keep out of my way."

She laughed. Her over-loud laughter was a constant irritation to him, like the accompanying display of shining white teeth . . . a toothpaste advertisement laugh. His irritation was increased when she mentioned that they would be together at Chantilly the following week-end. He made an ineffectual attempt to get out of going, announcing, the day before they were due to leave, that he intended to stay in Paris. The universal dismay caused by this decision surprised him, for not only did Louise beseech him to go with them, but so also did Brassart and Danielle. By the time his surprise had changed to disquiet, he had weakly given way.

He set out with Louise in the Dauphine, leaving Brassart and Danielle to drive alone in the D.S. Louise had made this decision, saying that she preferred her own car to her husband's. The Great B had raised no objection.

"She's giving us her blessing," said Danielle. "She knows I'm your mistress, but she couldn't care less now that she's got young Vincent."

"Oh, for Christ's sake, shut up!"

Brassart was driving very fast. He had slept badly and his head ached. Although he had lain awake thinking most of the night, his mind was still not clear about what he intended to do. He would have to wait.

"You know what they're going to do . . ." began Danielle.

"That's enough. I don't want to hear any more."

Since he had been able to see Danielle every day she had come to interest him less and less. Now it was hatred of Debosse that obsessed him. He was sure, however, that no one was aware of this, and Danielle's next comment startled him.

"You really hate that young man, don't you?"

"I don't hate him. I see him in the morning at the hospital

69

and at home in the evening. Having a stranger under one's feet all day and every day is enough to irritate anyone. Right?"

"Right," agreed Danielle gently.

Louise was happy. Her light summer frock made her look younger, and, gazing in her mirror that morning, she had felt she was both beautiful and desirable. Did Vincent find her desirable?

"Would you like to drive, Vincent?"

They were now out of Paris, and the sun was shining down on the tops of their heads. Vincent said he was a bad driver, he hadn't had enough practice, he'd never been able to afford a car. He added, however, that he did have a driving licence.

She let him take the wheel. It was as if she had offered him a magnificent and unexpected present. He smiled with real pleasure.

He started driving with extreme caution.

"You must get some practice, Vincent. I'll let you have the Dauphine for driving to the hospital."

He protested that she was too generous, but she insisted. She didn't mention that she had been highly alarmed ever since she had discovered that it was only a miracle which kept his ramshackle motor cycle together.

Her tenacity was disarming. "Twenty times a day she shows me she's in love with me," thought Vincent, "and twenty times a day I behave like an oaf. What can she hope for?"

Brassart's D.S. swept past them. Danielle waved. The Great B, sitting stiffly behind the wheel, didn't give them a glance.

"What are you thinking about, Vincent?"

"Your husband."

"Whatever for?"

He was wondering what the Great B had meant to Louise and whether he still sometimes visited his wife's bedroom at night.

"He's a great man, isn't he?"

She said she had a great admiration for Guillaume as a surgeon. Obviously she considered that Vincent was playing his role badly, but his shyness provoked her to increasing boldness.

"I expect you have lots of affairs?"

"No, Madame Brassart."

Vincent was driving faster now. His teeth clenched and a lock of hair falling over his forehead, he found he didn't care at all for the turn that the conversation was taking.

"You have a girl-friend, surely?"

"No, Madame Brassart."

He pressed his foot down more firmly on the accelerator, looking straight ahead, his cheeks crimson. "If she goes on like this I'll probably drive straight into a tree," he thought.

"That's difficult to believe, Vincent."

He took a deep breath. "There's something I find even more difficult to believe, Madame Brassart. I think that I've had the audacity to fall in love with you."

The week-end was a wonderful one for Louise. Vincent was no longer bothering to conceal his feelings. He abandoned his books for hours on end, walking at her side, holding her hand, touching her shyly. Despite the heat and his sunburn, he was the perfect lover.

These were the only memories Louise wanted to keep of those two days. However, it was difficult to forget certain words which Vincent had spoken. She would have preferred them more tender, less wild and strange. It seemed he was obsessed by fears which she thought quite absurd.

"You're in danger, Louise."

He had called her Louise, he had taken this—for him—enormous step. For her this was the most wonderful moment of a wonderful week-end.

"In danger? I don't understand."

He had talked about Danielle Fellegrini. He had been watching her. "I'm sorry, but it was necessary." He found her searching Louise's room. Danielle Fellegrini, he assured her, was up to something, and someone was going to suffer as a result.

"But why should it be me?"

"Louise, surely you understand!"

"I don't think there is anything to understand."

Her closed, expressionless face made it plain that she was tired of this "silly joke". But he persisted.

"She's your husband's mistress. That doesn't worry you, I know, but do you think she's going to be satisfied playing second fiddle?"

"What else can she expect?"

For a moment Vincent felt a sneaking sympathy with Danielle Fellegrini. He found Louise's blind complacency somewhat distasteful. However naïvely, she took the conventions of her own class for granted. She had never known financial insecurity, had never even experienced the anxieties of waiting for pay-day. She undoubtedly felt she had done the Great B a favour in marrying him. Did she perhaps think she was doing Danielle a favour by tolerating her as her husband's mistress?

"She might take your place," he said slowly. "She might become the second Madame Brassart."

Louise laughed quietly, insolently.

"Really, Vincent, you're quite mad!"

"Divorce isn't for dogs and cats, you know."

"And it isn't for the Brassarts either."

"Very well, let's forget about the whole thing."

"Yes, Vincent. I think that would be best."

Nevertheless, she had not forgotten.

For Guillaume the week-end had been a revelation. He didn't yet know whether to be relieved or disappointed, but he was now sure that he no longer loved Danielle. "Perhaps I never loved her. I wanted her body, it was like a drug to me . . . but nothing like love, really. In any case, out of bed she now bores me." In fact Danielle had been quite charming during this country week-end, but what good was that to him when his own wife was publicly humiliating him with that intolerable little upstart.

He had followed them into the woods, leaving Danielle alone in the house with a pile of letters, which she was typing faultlessly and uncomplainingly. It didn't occur to him that she was also taking the opportunity to pry into all the cupboards and all the drawers in all the rooms. He was no longer interested in Danielle, he no longer cared what she was doing; all his attention was now concentrated upon Louise and what he considered to be her fit of madness. He didn't pause to consider that his own behaviour might have struck an observer as unbalanced, to say the least. He had passed two whole days regretting that he had left his revolver in Paris, and had been on the point of driving back to collect it, but a vestige of common sense had restrained him. If he went to Paris with the sole object of getting his revolver that would be seen as nothing but premeditation.

His plan seemed to him, like the rest of his thinking, both clear and reasonable. "I could throw Debosse out, but Louise would go on seeing him. She would become his mistress—something she probably hasn't dared to do under my own roof. But these prim little prigs are capable of anything when they get the itch . . . they're worse than the others. They'll have it over your dead body if you're in their way." He realized he hated his wife; but less than he hated Debosse, who was simply an insect to be destroyed.

In the D.S. on the way back to Paris, Danielle was alarmed by his taciturnity and his brooding face.

"Aren't you feeling well?"

"I've got problems."

"Your wife?"

"I don't give a damn about my wife."

He felt wary of Danielle. It was not only that he had ceased to love her—she was an embarrassing and incriminating witness. He was hoping to be rid of her as soon as possible.

She had said nothing to let slip that she knew exactly how his mind was working. She continued to adhere to her policy of watchful diplomacy. "He thinks he doesn't love me any more because his wife is being unfaithful to him. Typical! But what men like him think or don't think doesn't matter. All that matters is to manoeuvre him step by step into a position from which there will be no escape."

All the same, she thought it worth while mentioning that their child was to be born in six months' time.

"It doesn't show," he said absently.

He made no further comment, and she didn't pursue the subject.

9

Since he had been driving to the hospital in the Dauphine, Vincent had taken to smoking in the morning again. This was not strictly a gesture of independence, it was also a sort of act of defiance, helping him to forget the humiliations Brassart had heaped upon him.

He was remembering them as he started the car that morning. Eight o'clock. Since he had been living in the Place Malesherbes he had been arriving rather earlier at the hospital, a good fifteen minutes before Brassart, at all events. With a cigarette as yet unlit between two fingers, driving gently down the busy Avenue de Villiers, Vincent reflected that Brassart would probably soon have good reason to hate him.

Suddenly he heard a police whistle. He thought at first that it was intended for the Aronde that had just passed him, but the *agent* persisted. He was waving the Dauphine down. Suddenly alarmed, Vincent braked sharply, felt the car skid, but straightened her up and stopped at the kerbside.

As he got out, he realized there was something wrong with the damned car—she had a peculiar, lop-sided look, but he didn't immediately spot the trouble. The *agent* pointed it out.

"You've got a flat tyre. Rear off-side. Let's see your licence."

Vincent held out his licence, lit a cigarette and bent down, wondering how the devil he was going to change the wheel. He had never been much good at that sort of thing.

"A practical joke!" he murmured, dragging out the bag of tools.

"You think it's a joke, do you."

74

The *agent* was examining his papers attentively, nodding sagely as he noticed that the car belonged to a woman and not to Vincent.

"Women are often careless about mechanical details," commented Vincent as he struggled with a bolt.

"You call that a mechanical detail?"

He handed back the papers. He was a man of about forty with large, very blue eyes that focused on Vincent's face like twin spotlights.

"Well, it certainly wasn't me who let the tyre down."

A small crowd had already gathered and a man in a cap was offering advice in a bantering tone. The jack was rusty. Vincent was sweating freely and the car wasn't rising an inch.

"You can't stop here all day," said the *agent*. "If you can't change your own wheel you'd better 'phone a garage."

He didn't care for doctors. In the past ten years he'd seen a lot of them, none of them any good. At the moment his blasted piles were hurting him, and a fat lot of good it had done going to the doctor. He'd paid out enough money to doctors to have bought himself a car, and he was a man who knew how to look after a car.

"I'll give you a hand," said the man in the cap.

He took the jack. Vincent thanked him, stood up, stamped out his cigarette, mopped his forehead and took off his jacket. It was as he was placing it on the back seat that he saw the container. A slim metal cylinder about the length of a baby's bottle. It had been pushed under the arm-rest and it looked harmless and forgotten.

Forgotten? Vincent's face turned pale as he picked up this forgotten object, for the container had not been hermetically sealed. The gas was escaping very slowly, almost imperceptibly.

"If I'd lit my cigarette . . . bang! The car would have blown up and me with it."

There was no possibility of doubt—the cylinder contained the most explosive of all anaesthetics—cyclopropane. He screwed the top on tightly with trembling hands.

"Well, that's that . . . for the moment. Now there's only the matter of changing the wheel."

He had forgotten to thank the man in the cap. He could think only that someone had put that container in the car with the idea that . . . It was, in fact, pure luck that he was still alive.

"If I'd lit my cigarette before getting out of the Dauphine, if . . ."

"What's that you've got there?"

The *agent* had come back and was looking in turn at Vincent's pale face and at the metal cylinder he was hugging to his chest.

"Sterile syringes," snapped Vincent. "In surgical spirit."

He wondered how he was going to get rid of the cyclopropane. It was impossible to take it back to the flat because it was now twenty-past eight and he hadn't the time. And if he did, he'd have to explain it all to Louise. He swore silently. Perhaps it was Louise whom someone had hoped to kill. After all, no one knew that she had lent him the car . . . no one, except Brassart.

"You'd better get a move on."

The *agent* was irritating him by walking round the Dauphine and then standing right behind him. Before he began to change the wheel, Vincent thrust the cylinder inside his brief-case and then pushed the case into the boot. When at last he was able to drive off, the *agent* was growling that there were a number of young men who'd never changed a wheel in their lives, but who were allowed to play around with the human body in hospitals.

Finally Vincent decided to give the cyclopropane to one of the anaesthetists' assistants who disliked the Great B as much as he did himself.

"I found this lying around in the doctors' cloakroom," he said casually. "The top had been loosened. A joke, I suppose."

"A joke! A very dangerous joke! If you want my opinion, I'd say someone was trying to steal it. They're getting to be a thieving lot round here—they'll pinch anything."

"Yes. They'll pinch anything," Vincent repeated stupidly.

He was still feeling quite dazed. The more he thought, the more confused his mind became. One thing alone was perfectly clear: the bottle couldn't have been taken directly from the hospital to the Dauphine. He had gone back to the Place Malesherbes at about 12.30 the previous afternoon and he had

76

been smoking as he drove. If the cyclopropane had been there then, there would have been an explosion. From one o'clock that afternoon the car had been parked in the street. No one had used it. Therefore the container must have been placed there, and the cap deliberately loosened during the night, or more probably first thing that morning. Brassart? Vincent ceased abruptly to think. His mind, as if paralysed with fear, refused to answer either yes or no.

Brassart made no comment on his late arrival, and when Vincent met him at midday in the courtyard he greeted him genially enough.

"Can I give you a lift back, Debosse?"

It was the first time he had ever made such an offer.

"No, thank you, sir."

"No? Why not?"

"I have the Dauphine, sir."

"What Dauphine?"

"Your . . . your wife's, sir."

"Oh, I see. I didn't know that."

He had known perfectly well.

Vincent remembered that the previous evening Brassart had not dined at home, he had returned very late. He no longer felt badly about suspecting Brassart. "All the same, though," he said to himself as he climbed into the Dauphine, "putting a cylinder of cyclopropane into a car and then loosening the top with the near certainty of someone's getting killed . . . it's a bit much."

Perhaps Brassart was going off his head. Perhaps he was already mad. That sort of psychosis was quite well known. The patient's behaviour is apparently normal and his relatives fail to notice anything unusual, then suddenly he betrays himself. . .

"I don't know . . . it's more likely I'm going mad myself."

He sat in the car, letting the engine run. His head was aching and he was lost in his speculations.

"One, Brassart hates me. Two, he invites me to stay with him. Why? Because he wants something from me. Three, I think I know what he expects: some false move on the part of his wife—a false move he expects me to provoke. Conclusion:

he's quite right. She and I are on a very slippery slope. But he isn't satisfied. He tries to engineer a very sticky end for me, and takes quite unnecessary risks into the bargain."

He let in the clutch and drove off, continuing his speculations, but considering Danielle Fellegrini in the role of the would-be murderer. His conclusions were, however, just as puzzling. Danielle Fellegrini's objective was quite simple. She wanted to marry Brassart. Why then should she wish to murder a young doctor who was causing her no trouble at all?

He had just reached the Place Malesherbes when all the pieces of the jigsaw seemed suddenly to fit together. Danielle Fellegrini certainly didn't know he was using the Dauphine. Brassart told her a great many things, but there was no reason why he should have told her that. So Louise was her prospective victim.

But how had Danielle got hold of the cylinder? Vincent recalled having heard her talking about the clinic at Meudon where Brassart operated one day a week from nine in the morning until midnight. The Great B could well have taken her there and left her in a room adjoining the operating theatre. Everyone knew that it was very easy to steal almost anything from a clinic, particularly at night. With her habit of ferreting everywhere, Danielle could easily have got hold of the cylinder.

The lift clattered to a standstill. Vincent opened the gate quickly and dived into the flat.

He was taking a shower when Marie knocked to tell him that lunch was served. He was sure that he wouldn't be able to eat anything, but as he could think of no valid excuse for remaining in his room he put on a fresh shirt and went down to join Louise. She was looking very gentle, very innocent, beyond suspicion, but Vincent's heart missed a beat. Supposing it was she . . . Louise? In his mind's eye he saw her in her quietly expensive coat, with a neat, prim hat on her pretty head, going to visit "her" patients at the hospital. Yes, she also had "her" patients, "her" visiting days, and in consequence she had free access to every part of the hospital. It would be even easier for her than for Danielle Fellegrini to filch a cylinder of cyclopropane.

"No. That's not possible. I really am going out of my mind."

"Are you all right, Vincent?" she was asking.

"Louise. . . I must talk to you. It's terribly important."

At that moment, Brassart came in and kissed his wife on the forehead, not even glancing at Vincent. Lunch seemed interminable to Vincent. He simply didn't know what to think.

"Danielle steals the cyclopropane. Fine. Nothing improbable about that. But sooner or later Brassart must learn that a container is missing, and that it disappeared the evening when Danielle was at the clinic. All the anaesthetists and all the dressers have to check their stocks and keep the surgeon informed. Therefore Brassart must know what happened, but he says nothing. So it must have been me who was meant to die, because the Great B knew I was using the Dauphine."

"Vincent, are you listening?"

"Yes . . . no . . . I'm sorry."

"Is something the matter? You've hardly eaten anything."

"I'm not very hungry."

Brassart had stood up. For some days now he had been having his coffee in the study. As soon as they were alone, Vincent told Louise what had happened that morning. He told her everything, but when he had finished, it still sounded a most improbable story.

"I can't believe it," murmured Louise.

She didn't seem alarmed—merely intrigued. Vincent suspected that if she did feel any fear, it was probably simply because she thought he was losing his reason.

"It's true, Louise. Do you think I'd invent such a story?"

She assured him that she didn't think that, but she added nothing further. Her silence and her composure baffled him.

"Perhaps the police should be called in," he muttered.

"Oh, you're incorrigible, Vincent. Do you want to make trouble for yourself?"

"It seems as if trouble is being made for me already! Do face the facts, Louise. You're in danger, or else I'm in danger, or most probably we both are. We must do something."

"All we can do is forget all about it."

Her voice was still soft and calm, but her smile was less

candid than he had previously known it. It was as if she were smiling to disguise her true feelings.

He stood up. He was going to think things over . . . again and again. In the end he would surely find a perfectly simple, logical, feasible explanation.

"I'm going to my room."

"I'll come with you."

"You aren't thinking . . ."

She followed him out of the room. Poor Vincent! He seemed so vulnerable, so defenceless. After all, he *could* have been killed! That container of . . . what was it called? That container must have been put there by one of the young doctors as a silly joke. Guillaume had told her once how, in his student days, he and his friends had got up to all sorts of stupid tricks. That's what young doctors were like—always up to something. Vincent was different. He didn't have much sense of humour. He was always fearing the worst and dramatizing things. Not that she was complaining, of course . . . she loved him precisely because he was different from the rest.

Not for a moment did she think that she herself might have suffered as a result of the practical joke. Although she took crime plays on television quite seriously she didn't really believe that the violent deaths she read about in the newspapers ever happened in real life. Like divorce, violent death simply didn't happen, in her family at least.

Vincent remained standing, feeling awkward and angry. She asked him to sit down. He pushed an easy chair forward for her and then sat down on the edge of the bed, fearful that Brassart might open the door and surprise them.

"Louise, what are you going to do about all this?"

"Would you like me to speak to Guillaume about it?"

He shrugged his shoulders in desperation. Either she really didn't understand, or she was refusing to understand. Either way, there was nothing to be done. He could have smacked her.

"That would be plain idiotic," he said sharply.

"Why? Guillaume would find out who at the hospital had been so silly as to put the container in the car."

"And suppose your husband was the joker?"

She smiled disbelievingly and walked over to the bed.

"You can't be serious!"

"Face the facts, Louise. Your husband hates me and . . ."

"If he hated you he wouldn't have wanted you to live with us."

"I've been asked here to play a role. I didn't know what it was when I first came, but you've helped me to improvise quite a few of the right lines."

She had sat down on the bed, putting one hand on his shoulder. She couldn't resist doing this, she needed to touch him. "It's like I used to feel with the children when they were small," she reflected, not without a trace of irony.

"What do you mean?"

She genuinely hadn't grasped what he meant. Indeed she had not really been listening to him. She was fascinated by his face. A beautiful face. But this time she couldn't avoid hearing him because he was shouting.

"Your husband is waiting for me to become your lover."

"You mean that's what he wants?"

"He may not want it himself, but his secretary—his mistress —she wants it with all her heart. Now do you understand?"

She shook her head. She didn't want to understand. It seemed to her simply that Vincent was seizing on a silly and unworthy excuse for eluding her.

Hoping to convince her, he took her by the shoulders, looked her straight in the eye, and pulled her close to him. This was probably what she wanted—to be treated like any other woman. He kissed her lips fiercely, but without any real pleasure. She had disappointed him.

Her own pleasure was intense, and she would have gone all the way with him, but he looked so afraid. Breathing quickly, she began to stroke his face.

Vincent felt ashamed. "I can't forget that next year I'm going to need her husband. I can't think of anything but the *Internat*. It's shameful and stupid, but that's how I am."

He laughed roughly.

"This is madness," he said.

"No," she replied. "We love each other."

"But there's so much else on our minds, Louise—this morning I might have died."

The evening was like so many others. Brassart had obliged them to dine quickly. He had an operation at Meudon and wouldn't be back till late. Louise and Vincent had spent a few moments on the terrace and he had prevented her only with difficulty from coming into his room. For some time the medical journals had been accumulating unread on his desk, and his books had been pushed away out of sight in the cupboard.

At midnight he went to bed, switched off the light, and thought about Louise. They were alone in the flat, just the two of them, the servants' rooms being on the sixth floor. She was probably hoping for him to come to her. Probably she had waited for him every night. She had made no secret of her willingness to become his mistress. He himself was by no means reluctant—he was, quite simply, afraid. He realized this was probably very foolish, and the nervous tension caused by conflicting fears and desires was beginning to tell on him. Brassart must be vastly amused . . . "will he, won't he?" On the other hand, if Brassart did have some plan in mind, he must be getting impatient. "Unless I've been wrong about everything from start to finish," thought Vincent. "Perhaps I've imagined it all."

At one o'clock in the morning when he fell into a heavy sleep, Louise had already been sleeping lightly for some time. She was awakened by an unusual noise. It was a light, hesitant, nervous step. She felt herself smiling. Vincent had plucked up his courage. Not wanting to alarm him by switching on the light, she lay motionless in the darkness, ready to throw her arms round him as he approached her bed.

The steps were exasperatingly slow. He must be hesitating. Now she could hear nothing except the rapid beating of her own heart. She wanted to spring out of bed . . . but must she lead him in like a child? The footsteps began again, and she sighed and waited. At last the door, which she never locked, opened slightly. He was certainly being careful. She waited with increasing impatience. Vincent was standing on the other side of the door. What was he waiting for?

She was just going to switch on the light when, abruptly, she stiffened. It was absurd, unbelievable, utterly stupid, but suddenly she felt terrified. Vincent's fears must be infectious . . . all those fantastic stories, his silly panics, and now she was in the same state of nerves.

But it wasn't Vincent standing behind the door. Abruptly she realized that he would never have had the courage. She had been a fool to imagine it was he.

The floor creaked and she huddled down under the bed-clothes, unable to cry out, unable to move, her body wet with perspiration and icy cold. It wasn't Vincent . . . but who was it? Perhaps . . . She didn't want to know. She didn't want to know anything. No! No! No!

The shot rang out. Deafening. She gulped in terror, motion-less beneath the sheets, hoping to be ignored, forgotten, trying to forget her own existence.

Vincent was having a nightmare. A man was firing at him and two others were holding him down. He couldn't shout or move. The noise was deafening, the revolver enormous. A blinding flash. He was dying, but he wouldn't suffer, he had never suffered.

By the time he was fully awake he was sweating and his teeth were chattering. *Was* it a nightmare?

He switched on the light, got up and stumbled to the bath-room. As he put his head under the shower, it dawned on him that a shot had really been fired. Someone had used a revolver somewhere in the flat, but only he and Louise were there.

Louise! Without bothering to snatch up his dressing-gown he ran along the corridor in his pyjamas, saw the door ajar, went in and switched on the light. The revolver shot had left an acrid smell in the air. Louise was still in bed, but she had pushed back the bedclothes. Her face on the pillow looked delicate, vulnerable, and her eyes were wide, fixed, glazed. He crossed the room swiftly and took her hand.

83

"Are you all right? Louise? What's happened?"

She was crying. Large, slow tears were running down her pale face. She was all right, she hadn't been hit, but she was frightened. Terribly frightened. She couldn't understand. A shot had been fired through the door, which someone had pushed open. But who?

"Who did it, Vincent? Who?"

The bullet had penetrated the wall about a foot above the head of the bed, a few inches from where Louise's head was now lying. A small chip of plaster, a little dust, and a loud bang, but no harm done. Vincent released her hand. Her assailant must have escaped by the service door. The concierge might have caught sight of him. They must call the police at once.

"We must call the police, Louise," he said urgently.

She nodded, staring at him with clouded eyes. He was trembling, scarcely daring to breathe. He felt hot and cold and his stomach was turning over.

"What's going on?"

It was Brassart, his face white and harassed, standing in the doorway. Vincent moved quickly away from the bed.

"Did you hear, Guillaume?" Louise whimpered.

"Hear what? I've just got in."

In a low, constrained, almost unrecognizable voice, Louise explained. Brassart listened, stroking the bridge of his nose. When Louise had finished, he shrugged. "Is that all?" he said unconcernedly.

"I'm going to call the police," declared Vincent.

"You'll do nothing until I tell you, Debosse! I suppose you've already searched the flat?"

"I haven't searched anywhere. I haven't had time. But if you think that the person who fired that shot is sitting waiting for us to look for him you must be mad. If we're going to catch whoever it was we'd better call the police quickly. That's our first job."

"No," said Brassart quietly, turning towards his wife.

Louise was wriggling nervously, her cheeks flushed.

"But Guillaume! I might have been killed," she protested. "If I hadn't slid down the bed I *would* have been killed."

84

"Nonsense, my dear! You mustn't be so melodramatic."

He picked up the cartridge-case which had rolled beneath a chair and put it in his pocket. Then he examined the wall at the spot where the bullet had struck. He was breathing heavily, his face tense, a cigarette in his hand. He looked worried, but he was brazening it out.

"It's just an ordinary burglary," he announced. "The fool probably thought you kept your jewellery in your bedroom."

He was accustomed to saying outrageous things which no one dared to challenge, but this time he had, he felt, surpassed himself.

"Of course!" said Vincent, sarcastically. "He waited carefully until your wife was in bed. Presumably it would have seemed too easy to come to her bedroom when no one was here. At about nine o'clock, for instance . . ."

"At nine o'clock the servants are still around," said Brassart nonchalantly.

"But they've left before ten and your wife is seldom in bed as early as that."

"You know my wife's habits," said Brassart pointedly. "A burglar would be less likely to be so well acquainted with them."

He was staring insolently at Vincent. "Impudent young ape," he thought. "Bastard! Do you think I'll let myself be usurped by a pathetic creature like you?"

"He seemed to know his way around the flat all right. He knew where to find Madame Brassart's room. This is a pretty big flat, you know. And, anyway, how did he get in?" demanded Vincent.

It was like it had been at the *Internat* examination: he could scarcely recognise his own voice. He kept thinking that they must call the police, not waste another minute. He ought to ignore Brassart, stop being afraid of the swine, behave like a normal, balanced adult. "But what in heaven's name have I done to get mixed up in all this?" he wondered helplessly.

"The burglar came in through the service door, obviously," said Brassart. "That's the shortest way to Louise's room. It would be child's play to force the lock. I'll go and check it now, and then we can all . . ."

"I'm going to call the police," repeated Vincent.

He hadn't time to take a step. Brassart had moved in front of him, barring his way to the door. He was half a head taller than the younger man, huge, immovable, terrifying.

"Listen to me, Debosse," said Brassart menacingly. "You've seen nothing, heard nothing. You were asleep. You're still asleep. You're probably dreaming. Don't move. I'll be back in a moment. Is that clear?"

While Brassart was out of the room, Vincent stared silently at Louise. He didn't dare go over to her side. He felt ashamed.

"I love you, Vincent. I don't understand what it's all about. It's absurd. But I love you, Vincent."

She lay still, one sun-tanned leg dangling out of bed, covered to the knee by her pink silk nightdress. When Brassart returned she withdrew her leg again under the sheets.

"I was right, of course," he said. "The door had been forced. He had broken the lock and knocked over a chair."

"I didn't hear anything," objected Louise.

Brassart shrugged and looked at his watch. He felt very tired.

"There weren't any other traces," he added.

"The police would find other traces," murmured Vincent, though he knew it was useless to argue.

Brassart didn't bother to reply. His hands in his pockets, he was reflecting that the police would have plenty to do the day they were called in to investigate the murder of Debosse.

Louise had sat up, still looking very pale. A simple, obvious idea had just occurred to her. The person who had tried to kill her once, and failed, might try again.

"You *must* call the police, Guillaume," she implored. "Guillaume, you must!"

He stared at her in surprise. She had never asked him for help or protection—she had always been composed, invulnerable, no tears, no fuss—and now he couldn't respond to her need.

"I'm frightened, Guillaume," she repeated. "I shan't ever feel safe again."

86

He sat down on her bed, taking her hand in his, trying to show a tenderness he no longer felt.

"There's nothing to worry about, my dear. Tomorrow I'll have all the locks changed."

"But why don't we call the police?" she insisted, tearfully.

He smiled. He was beginning to feel angry.

"What point would there be?" he said curtly. "Nothing has been stolen, nobody has been hurt. If I call the police, there's only a chance in a thousand of their catching the man, but they would certainly make our lives a misery. Have you ever had any dealings with the police? No? They're bastards. They pry into everything, they leave no one's private business alone. They'll do anything, no matter whose reputation is at stake. You must think of your father . . ."

"You can't *not* call them," exclaimed Vincent. "If you don't call them, you can be sure the neighbours will."

He had raised his voice. A lock of hair hung over his forehead and his eyes were haggard. He was addressing the nape of Brassart's thick neck.

Brassart turned and stared at him. He said nothing but Vincent could read his thoughts in his small grey eyes: "If you persist, Debosse, I'll destroy you. I'm in my own house, and the fact that you're here at all is due only to the generosity or stupidity of my wife, and neither will last for ever. You'd do best to make yourself scarce and forget everything you've seen. If not, the police will indeed be called, and what will they make of your presence here? What will they think are your relations with my wife? What conclusions will they draw when they learn you were alone with her in this flat when the shot was fired? My word against yours, Debosse . . . which of us will they believe would you think?"

"If there's nothing more I can do, I'm going back to bed," said Vincent. "Goodnight."

"Goodnight, Debosse."

Louise said nothing. She was looking down at the hand she had withdrawn from Guillaume's clasp.

In the darkness Vincent lay thinking about Brassart and the possible reasons for his extraordinary behaviour. His pretexts for not calling the police were nothing short of ridiculous, not to be taken seriously for a moment. Vincent would have laughed in his face if he hadn't been near to tears. Had Brassart himself tried to shoot his own wife?

One, Brassart had come in three or four minutes after the shot was fired—the time needed to go down the service stairs, cross the courtyard, come in through the front door, and take the lift to the fifth floor to reach Louise's room again. Two, Brassart had picked up the cartridge-case and put it in his pocket. No doubt he would do the same with the bullet he would cut out of the wall. A surgical operation! In short, all traces of the shot would have disappeared the next day. Perhaps the revolver was his own? If he had one. Three, contrary to all reason and prudence, he had refused to send for the police, as if they didn't know when they had to wear kid-gloves, as everyone did when dealing with people like the Great B. Conclusion: either Brassart had fired the shot himself, or else he was protecting the person who had fired it. This led Vincent back to the problem posed a few days earlier by the cyclopropane incident, with the difference that this time it was clear that Louise alone was the intended victim.

But if Brassart wished to kill his wife, he had at his disposal other means that were much less conspicuous and far more certain. Yes, far more certain.

Eventually, with the aid of sleeping pills, Vincent succeeded in dismissing all these thoughts from his mind until dawn. Only hours later, when he was getting up, did it occur to him that he should have left the flat, parted from the Brassarts for ever, and found himself somewhere to live as far as possible from the Place Malesherbes; and by then it was too late, for as he returned from the bathroom he felt an unusual weight in the right-hand pocket of his dressing-gown. The Mauser he drew out was black and shining. He stood stock still, stupefied, holding it awkwardly in his hand. It was several seconds before he realized what it was.

His first reaction was to go to Brassart and tell him, but he had taken hardly a step along the corridor when he realized that this was the last thing he should do. Louise! Louise would be terrified. She would probably 'phone the police, and now he felt too shaken to face their enquiries. With the Mauser wrapped in a newspaper inside his brief-case, he left at eight o'clock without having seen either Louise or Brassart.

Could it be someone's idea of a joke? No, it couldn't . . . He was talking to himself at the wheel of the Dauphine. One bullet was missing from the revolver—he had checked. How could he go into a *commissariat* and even begin to explain. "Listen! Last night someone tried to shoot Madame Brassart. I live in the flat with Guillaume Brassart, the famous surgeon, the son-in-law of Professor Gladieux, and his wife. This morning there was this revolver in my dressing-gown pocket. Who am I? Vincent Debosse, medical student. I have two hundred and fifty francs a month to live on, my mother is dead, and I've never known my father."

No, he couldn't go to the police with this story. He would keep the revolver, and put it in a safe place. He had all morning to decide where.

Brassart didn't join them for lunch. Vincent learned from Louise that the Great B had given the concierge and the servants an official account of the murder attempt. While he was cleaning his revolver a shot had been fired accidentally. No one had been hurt, and the incident was now closed.

"In any case, the servants hadn't heard anything," added Louise. "Nor had the concierge."

"And where is your husband's revolver?" asked Vincent.

"I don't know where he keeps it. It's an army revolver. He's shown it to me several times."

"He ought not to mislay it . . . you never know, the police may still get to hear of this."

"Oh, don't go on about the police . . ."

"You went on about the police yourself last night."

"Yes, but I was frightened then."

She looked pale and tired, and under her eyes were dark rings not entirely concealed by her make-up. He longed to take her in his arms and comfort her. There was no point in obliging her to share his own anxieties, or in frightening her still more by telling her about the revolver he had found in the pocket of his dressing-gown.

"Louise, I love you," he said instead.

"Be careful . . . Marie's coming back."

Marie brought in the cheeseboard and Louise began talking about a film she had watched recently on television. He realized suddenly that if he were to become her lover he would hear the words "be careful" very often. At present she was ready to take immense risks, certainly, but that was probably simply because he was hanging back, because she was unsure of him, or, possibly, because she was finding it intolerable that he existed as her lover only in her own imagination. Unless, of course, she really loved him . . .

It seemed as if she did. She followed him to his room and clung to him. Suddenly she had tears in her eyes. Was she too old for him, not attractive any more? Then as she dried her eyes she kissed him and repeated that she loved him, she was beside herself with love for him. Vincent felt for the first time in his life that he knew very little about women.

"You aren't still frightened?" he asked gently.

"Frightened? Why should I be frightened?"

He could have hit her. "One day I will hit her, and I'll feel all the better for it, and so, perhaps, will she."

He was sitting at her feet and she smiled, relaxing completely.

"It's more serious than you realize, Louise. It wasn't a burglar last night—it was someone who knows you very well."

"Oh, goodness, Vincent . . . don't let's go over it all again! I admit I was frightened at the time, but since then I've thought it over. It must have been a burglar. I do have some very nice jewellery, after all, and that sort of thing gets known."

"Louise, if you're thinking it over at all, why not think straight? No one was after your jewellery when the cyclopropane cylinder was put in the Dauphine. These were two attempts at

90

murder, they were the work of one and the same person, and they were almost certainly attempts to murder *you*."

"I think the cylinder business was just a joke—I've told you so before."

She was stroking his hair, and thinking that he said tiresome, worrying things, but was nevertheless irresistibly charming—at least to her.

"Louise! You're living in a dream-world, and if you don't wake up it'll cost you your life or me mine."

She shrugged impatiently, and stood up, turning away to light a cigarette. How silly he was!

"Very well, Vincent. Perhaps I *am* in danger. But Guillaume is having all the locks changed and he's installing an alarm system. What more can we do?"

"Tell the police."

She looked at him as if he were an obstinate child.

"As Guillaume said—and you were there at the time—calling the police would be pointless. It would be a great nuisance for us all."

"Guillaume! Guillaume! Forgive me, Louise, if I sound as if I were your lover. I don't want to speak badly of your husband, but, believe me, you shouldn't take it for granted that he's always right."

She sat smoking, smoothing her hair into place. Then she leaned towards him.

"You haven't been to the police, have you, Vincent?"

"I haven't done anything."

She lifted his chin with her hand and he looked up into her large, dark eyes, which were surveying him without emotion. He would never understand her. A moment before she had been crying over nothing, but now, contemplating events that chilled his own spine, she could remain apparently unperturbed.

"Don't look at me like that, Louise. God, these last few days have been unbearable! I don't know what I'm at—or what I might do next."

IO

"It's quite simple. Yesterday morning that damned revolver was in the drawer of my desk—I saw it there—and last night it had gone. In the meantime, someone tries to shoot my wife."

Brassart wasn't eating. He was watching her. With eyes lowered, Danielle was attacking her food with relish.

"You're terrific when you talk about 'my wife'—you talk in quotes. Your wife reads too many detective novels, and she lives too much in her imaginary affair with Debosse. She probably invented the whole thing."

"She didn't invent anything. I found the bullet and the cartridge-case."

"Perhaps Debosse tried to shoot her?"

"He's in love with her."

"Precisely."

"What do you mean—precisely?"

"He may have tried to kill her precisely because he's in love with her and it's hopeless. Love's a complicated business, you know. At least, you should know . . ."

"I don't care much for your taste in jokes," he said with studied calm.

"I don't care for yours, either. They're too far-fetched. Your wife is alone in the flat with her lover—oh, there's no need to look like that . . . I apologize, maybe he isn't her lover yet. Anyway, your revolver disappears. A burglar tries to shoot your wife, misses, and vanishes. If that sounds a likely tale to you, why don't you run and tell the police?"

"I want to find out who stole my Mauser."

He was staring over Danielle's bare shoulder at something invisible except to himself.

"Anyone might have taken it," she said. "Debosse, the servants, your wife."

"You."

"Yes, but I didn't take it. I wasn't alone in your study for a single minute yesterday. You were there all the time, if you remember."

"My memory isn't very good."

"You'd better try to improve it, then, because there's one person the police will certainly be interested in, and that's you. You're saying someone stole your revolver. Right? And no one has been able to prove they didn't . . . so far!"

"Are you still joking?"

"Perhaps. Perhaps not."

He looked at her with growing irritation. She was smiling, beautiful, arrogant, voracious. She had just finished the large chocolate cake which Guillaume hadn't been able to touch.

"Have you ever wanted to kill anyone?"

"Yes, of course. You know that perfectly well," she answered without hesitation or embarrassment. He felt baffled.

"But that was simply a daydream," she went on easily. "Or a nightmare, rather. Since then I've learned how to wait. I'm still waiting."

"What are you driving at?"

"Nothing. It's you who are worried. You've lost your revolver. If it's disappeared, that's serious, isn't it? A revolver's useful in a *crime passionnel*."

He just managed to stop himself from striking her. He needed to keep calm.

"Coffee?"

He shook his head, took the bottle of wine and refilled his glass. Damned bitch. He was almost certain that she had taken the revolver from the drawer of his desk, come to the flat the previous evening, and let herself in by the service door. A spare key was kept permanently on a hook in the kitchen. To steal this during the day, to use it in the evening and put it back before leaving, shutting the door behind her . . . all that would have been child's play. Danielle was a child, in a way. She did childish things. That business of the cylinder, for instance . . . it was lucky Louise had told him about it, and that neither she nor Debosse had guessed who had been responsible. He must be careful not to alarm her. He must treat her like a mad woman, with great caution.

She was still smiling.

"You look like a soul in torment. Indigestion?"

"No."

"Don't you love me any more?"

"Have I said that?"

She realized she must be on her guard. She had already said too many foolish things, and it would be better now if she kept quiet. As she stood up to clear the table her eyes met his and she saw that she had gone too far. She took the plates into the kitchen, piled them in the sink, and went to shut herself in the bathroom. This was her favourite corner, a decorated nightmare, black-tiled from floor to ceiling, that had cost a small fortune. Seated on the edge of the bath, she mulled over the events of the recent past. She had blundered first with the cyclopropane, and then with the revolver shot. She had been a fool who had lost her head. Indeed, she had probably lost everything. Guillaume would never marry her now, she was sure of that. Perhaps in her heart of hearts she had always known it. The real obstacle to the marriage wasn't Louise, but herself, the person she was—a nobody—and it was this she found intolerable. It was this reluctant self-knowledge that was driving her on, forcing her deeper and deeper into the mire.

He was calling her. It was two-thirty. She would go with him to the Place Malesherbes and spend the afternoon typing his letters. She would stay with him until seven in the evening. In future they would hardly ever be apart. They hated each other.

"Are you ready?"

"I'll just scribble a note for the cleaner and then I'll be with you."

He grimaced as he noticed her perfume. She used too much. She was altogether too much, but he couldn't blame her. She was just an unhappy, neurotic, unbalanced woman—with good reason, perhaps. He had felt recently that he might be heading for a breakdown himself. A claustrophobic situation, nerve-racking. No one was really to blame—not Louise, not Debosse, especially not Danielle, and certainly not himself. Life had played a lousy, cheating trick on them all. Their drama was moving relentlessly to its climax, so why try to resist? He was obsessed by murder as if it were a challenge. He didn't really wish to kill, but he no longer had any choice. Perhaps Danielle was caught up in a similar psychological process. But Danielle was a fool. She was good for nothing except to create chaos, and she was expecting his child. She must be eliminated.

He wondered suddenly how long it was since they had last made love. Five days? Six? Yes, six! He smiled. Not so long ago he hadn't been able to look at her without aching to take her in his arms, and now he didn't even remember to desire her. That was excellent. He was ready. Ready to say: "It's all over. You're free. I'm free. We're too honest to talk nonsense about remaining good friends, but I'll help you financially. I'll see the child is all right. You've nothing to worry about. I won't write again, and I'll never come back."

He was ready, but when she joined him he took her arm and said nothing. Possibly he had waited too long. For once he was entirely frank with himself. Danielle frightened him.

On the first Saturday in the month the Brassart children arrived at the Place Malesherbes towards midday, and, after a quick lunch, the whole family left for Chantilly.

Danielle had the day off, and Vincent was staying in Paris in spite of Louise's efforts to persuade him to accompany them. She wanted the children to get to know him better, she said. They would soon accept him and love him—why not?—like a big brother.

"Don't be silly, Louise. And what about your husband?"

"Guillaume?"

"Your husband isn't likely to start accepting me as his eldest son, is he?"

"Perhaps not. But two days is such a long time without you."

"You'll have the boys."

"Yes."

She felt no remorse. "I love my children, of course. I'll always have them to love, but I haven't much time to love you." Although her father confessor had admonished her and urged her to renounce this dangerous passion, she was at peace with herself. Nothing could stop her loving Vincent. He had been sent to her—a gift from heaven.

On the eve of leaving for Chantilly with the children, however, she had a fright. She was in Vincent's room, trying once more to persuade him to come with them; but he had refused, and was sitting, pale, wretched and obstinate as ever, on the bed. She went over to him and put her arms round him, then she lay back, pulling him close to her and kissing him fiercely.

They didn't hear Danielle knock at the door, though she insisted that she had. "Oh, I'm sorry . . . excuse me! I didn't realize . . ."

She stood in the doorway, a slender silhouette with red hair, smiling triumphantly. Louise was sitting up now, more embarrassed than either of the others. There were beads of perspiration on her forehead. Danielle pretended to have noticed nothing and turned casually to Vincent who had crossed the room and was making no effort to conceal his annoyance.

"What d'you want?" he demanded.

"I was wondering if you could help me with a word I don't know in this article Monsieur Brassart has asked me to type. May I show you?"

She was holding out a sheet of paper. Vincent took it without looking at it.

"There are medical dictionaries in the flat," he said.

"Yes, but they're all in Monsieur Brassart's consulting room, and he has a patient with him."

He wanted to screw up the paper she had given him and hurl it at her. But he thought of Louise, of the situation they were in, and he resigned himself to giving Danielle the help she had asked.

"Thank you so much. How kind of you," she said finally.

"Not at all," he answered stiffly.

He handed the paper back to her and steered her firmly towards the door, which he opened.

"Next time, call me on the intercom—that's what it's for."

"I didn't think. I'm so sorry. And thank you again."

He closed the door and mopped his forehead. "She certainly caught us that time," he thought as he returned to Louise, who was sitting silent and motionless.

"Well, she won that round," he commented.

"She hasn't won anything and she isn't going to," said Louise in a strange, choked voice. "Guillaume will have to choose whether to believe her or me, and he won't hesitate . . ."

"No. He'll believe her."

She laughed angrily.

"You're a child, Vincent. Do stop worrying for nothing. I'm not afraid, am I?"

On Sunday he was alone in the flat, free to potter, to remain unwashed, to eat sandwiches and watch the television. He could even have settled down to some work, but this he carefully avoided.

As he was returning to his own room, the door-bell sounded: two short rings. Before opening the door, he buttoned up his shirt. It was none too clean, and the collar and cuffs were frayed.

Danielle Fellegrini was standing outside, wearing a head-scarf.

"I won't beat about the bush," she said immediately. "I've come to talk to you."

"There's nothing I want to discuss with you."

She was wearing fawn slacks and a light sweater and she looked as if she had just got back from the country. She took off the scarf and walked past Vincent into a room she hardly knew . . . the waiting-room.

"It's terribly gloomy in here, isn't it? Almost monastic. Not even a knick-knack."

"Knick-knacks, and even pictures, tend to get taken away by patients as souvenirs. Surely you knew that?"

"Surely not from the waiting-room of a famous surgeon?"

"Especially from the waiting-room of a famous surgeon. His patients probably think that as they're so well able to pay, no one will suspect them. Well, what is it? I'm busy."

"I told you. I want to talk to you."

"Carry on, then, but be quick about it."

She sat down in an armchair, crossed her legs and lit a cigarette.

"You're a curious young man. Not like most men."

"Nobody is like anyone else. You didn't come here to tell me that. And there's an ashtray just behind you—this isn't a café."

"No. We're both at home here, aren't we? You do feel at home with me, don't you?"

"What's the game? I'm warning you . . . I've been wanting to box your ears for a long time now."

"Yes, I know," she said, offering him a cigarette. "But let's talk calmly. Sit down, I won't bite you."

But he continued to stand, stooping, his hands in the pockets of his jeans, his eyes averted.

She said she was sorry there had been bad feeling between them. She had done her best to be friends, but he had always rebuffed her. Madame Brassart was much friendlier, much more understanding, even though she was rather distant.

"You don't expect her to throw her arms round your neck, do you? Everyone knows what you are to her husband, and no one is blaming you. But no one's going to congratulate you either."

"I don't expect anything. I just wish that Madame Brassart would see her own situation as realistically as she sees mine. I'm talking about the role *you* play in her life, of course."

"Go ahead. I'm listening," he said calmly.

She stood up and walked across to him. Her arms folded, a cigarette between her lips, she gazed at him thoughtfully.

"Don't be childish. I don't give a damn myself about your making love to Madame Brassart, but Guillaume wouldn't be pleased. If he found out you'd be likely to come off rather badly . . . and that's putting it mildly."

"So that's it, is it? Vulgar blackmail. I'd have expected you to be more clever than that."

"Not blackmail. Just a friendly warning—a little disinterested advice. Let's say it's because I've always had a soft spot for you."

"And I've some advice for you, too. Next time you're trying to commit the perfect crime, don't leave your personal possessions in someone else's car."

"I don't follow you."

"You will. I drive Madame Brassart's Dauphine almost every day. It so happened, one morning, that I found something very dangerous in that car—a container of cyclopropane, to be precise. A container which someone had failed to seal."

"What on earth are you talking about?"

She smiled and looked him straight in the eyes. Possibly she was cleverer than he had thought.

"A container of cyclopropane is more or less anonymous, of course," he went on. "But the contents of a woman's handbag are different . . . they can be identified more easily."

"Oh, for heaven's sake . . . I haven't the faintest idea what you're talking about. Stop playing detectives, you're wasting your time. I've nothing on my conscience."

He sighed. He had not been very subtle. Only the heroines of cheap detective stories leave monogrammed powder-compacts at the scene of the crime. He was out of his depth. She was right. He was wasting his time.

"Don't let me detain you, then. I've got work to do."

She had gone to sit down again, and was watching him intently. If he suspected her, it might prove catastrophic for her future.

"Very well. I shan't take up much of your time. You're taking a big chance, not only with your career but with your neck. Brassart is going off his head. It's not just that he hates you, it's worse. He can't bear for you even to exist. Do you understand? And that's where I come in. I can protect you, I can help you, but I'm not putting up with your rudeness or your superior airs and graces. As long as Brassart thinks you're not his wife's lover, but simply her little weakness, you've a chance. But it only needs a word from me and you'll be for it."

"So it all depends on you, does it?"

"That's right. I've got eyes in my head and I've been using them, but I can be discreet if I'm asked nicely. That's what I wanted to tell you. And now I'll leave you in peace."

He went with her to the door. Suddenly she laughed.

"I was just thinking . . . perhaps there's been some mis-mating in our foursome. You're young and good-looking, and I'm not exactly old and plain. Maybe we're made for each other?"

"Love is irrational," he said. "Fortunately. Goodnight."

II

This was Danielle's third visit to Chantilly. She thought it might well be the last. She needed only to glance at Guillaume to feel sure that he was reaching breaking point and could control himself only with great difficulty. Sooner or later, he would crack. The previous evening, partly out of bravado and partly because she wanted to stop hoping for anything from this man she hated, she had told him the truth about the revolver shot and the cyclopropane. To her surprise, he had laughed. A huge, monstrous laugh.

They reached Chantilly before Louise and Vincent. Guillaume shut himself up in his bedroom immediately, saying he was tired and wanted to get some sleep. She could go for a walk in the woods or anywhere else, he didn't give a damn what she did. He didn't want to see her before six o'clock. *Ciao!*

She noticed that he had already drunk a great deal and was still drinking. He took a bottle of whisky with him into his bedroom. Danielle, sitting at the window of her own bedroom, saw Louise and Vincent arrive. Louise was wearing a print frock with a V neck and looked younger than usual. Her short, glossy hair was blowing in the wind.

Half-an-hour later, Louise emerged from the house wearing riding-breeches, and said a few words to Vincent who was setting out his books on a table in the shady part of the garden.

Danielle could see only his back, the delicate nape of his neck, and his thick brown hair. He had completely forgotten her existence. He was thinking about Louise, and about the peculiar way she had been behaving during the last few days: for long periods she had sat silent, showing extreme caution, then, suddenly, she had displayed her passion for him to the point of foolhardiness.

In the Dauphine she had put her arms round his neck while he was driving and kissed him very quickly on his cheeks, his lips and his forehead, disregarding the passing cars. With her lips pressed to his she had muttered: "I can't bear it. I'd do it here, now. It's killing me!"

A moment later she said miserably: "I suppose you don't want me. I'm too old for you."

Later again, as they reached the outskirts of Chantilly, she spoke quite calmly: "We mustn't be seen together too much this week-end. I'm not thinking just of myself, Vincent. It's for your sake, too. We must remember your career. We must be very careful."

Now she was being excessively careful. She'd scarcely spoken to him before going out riding. This evening, he felt sure, she would say she was tired and would go to bed early without insisting on coming to his room. But suppose she did come? Suppose she came and repeated what she had said earlier: "I can't bear it. It's killing me!" Well, it would make things easier if she kept away. "I can't bear it either," thought Vincent. "It's too much to ask any man, to go on like this."

An hour later he was still hunched over his books, but he wasn't studying. With the abruptness his mother had reproached him for when, as a child, he had suddenly startled her, he stood up and looked towards the house. Through the nylon curtain across a window on the first floor, he thought he had caught a glimpse of Danielle Fellegrini. He decided it must have been her. He would no doubt see her that evening at one of those crazy "family dinners". Then, suddenly, he realized that Danielle's bedroom didn't overlook the garden but the road. The figure he had seen was in Louise's bedroom.

He leapt to his feet and ran towards the house. Danielle was sitting in an armchair in the drawing-room, a book in her lap.

"Looking for something?"

"What were you doing in Madame Brassart's bedroom?"

He was furious, and out of breath. "The bitch was too quick for me," he thought angrily.

"You're crazy! The sun seems to have been too strong for you. I haven't been in Madame Brassart's bedroom ever."

There was no point in arguing. He might as well bang his head against a brick wall. In any case, he thought hopelessly, what could he do?

When Louise came back about five o'clock he didn't mention the incident to her. First, because he had decided that any attempt at serious discussion with the Brassarts was useless—their reactions simply made him feel upset and frustrated and stupid; and, secondly, because he had gone to Louise's room and found nothing and no one.

"You look tired, Vincent. Have you been working too hard?"

Louise was surveying him expressionlessly. She was smoking, and fanning the air in front of her face with one hand.

"I haven't been working. I've been thinking. Louise, I must go away. I can't go on like this. In any case, a situation like this is intolerable for everyone."

She looked aghast. She didn't answer but when he got up she followed him to his room. With tears in her eyes she begged him not to leave her. He meant everything to her, she'd have nothing left if he abandoned her.

His resolution weakened with every sentence she spoke, and with every half-hearted attempt he made to discourage her.

"Oh, for heaven's sake, leave me alone! I've told you a hundred times to face the facts. If you don't today, it'll soon be too late. I must go, not just for my own safety, but for yours . . . for your children's sake."

She brushed away her tears with the back of her hand and then stood up without a word. "I do love her," he thought fiercely. "I'm done for, she's done for, but I'm going to stay." He caught her in his arms, and they made love with haste and violence. He treated her roughly and without delicacy, perhaps hoping to frighten or disgust her; but if he had asked her what she felt she would have thought him unbelievably naïve.

At eight o'clock when Marie came to tell him that dinner was served, Vincent was lying on his bed reading a newspaper. Louise had gone back to her own room.

Before going downstairs, he switched on the bedside lamp and drew the curtains. While he was washing his hands and combing his hair, he was tormented by the feeling that there was something he had forgotten—something important.

He gazed at his reflection in the wardrobe mirror to be sure that he was properly dressed. He was wearing his old blue jeans with a brightly coloured sports shirt Louise had given him. No, whatever it was, it had nothing to do with his clothes. A moment before he'd almost got it . . . he'd have no peace until he put his finger on whatever it was.

As he shut the door of his room it almost came to him, but everyone was waiting for him, and dinner was served. He pushed the matter to the back of his mind.

Downstairs the others were already at table, the two women sitting opposite each other. Louise, expressionless, didn't look at him as he seated himself on her right. Before they had finished their meal she complained of having a migraine.

"Have you taken anything for it?" asked Brassart.

"No. I hadn't anything handy. Anyway, I'm frightened of all these pills people take nowadays."

Brassart shrugged and grimaced with distaste.

"You talk like a charwoman. Chemicals in one form or another are part of civilized life."

Danielle stood up.

"I'll go and fetch you something," she said. "I know all about headaches. I get them myself."

Brassart motioned her to be quiet and sit down.

"I'll go myself," he said.

He rose to his feet ponderously, like an old, fat man. Vincent thought that if anyone was ill in this house it was Brassart. He had aged unbelievably during the past few weeks. He was no longer the fine figure he used to be, histrionic and extrovert; he had turned almost overnight into an exhausted, elderly man.

He came back ten minutes later and laid two pink pills in front of his wife.

"I couldn't find what I wanted. I don't seem to be able to find anything these days. Take those and go up to bed."

Before standing up, Louise leaned towards Vincent. She whispered something rapidly, but he couldn't catch what she was saying. He didn't dare turn and watch her go. Again, he was tormented by the nagging feeling that there was something he ought to remember.

Dinner ended in silence. Brassart, who had been eating absent-mindedly, didn't seem put out by this. The moment he had swallowed his last mouthful of food he rose, giving Danielle and Vincent a wintry smile as he left them together.

"Do you play gin-rummy?" asked Danielle.

"I don't play any games."

He didn't know why he suddenly felt sorry for her. Her voice, perhaps. It was huskier than usual, as if she had a cold. Her eyes were swollen and red. Perhaps she had been crying? He imagined her alone with Brassart, putting up with his moods. With Louise, Brassart made some effort to mind his language, but Danielle was only his mistress. He probably treated her abominably. She was dependent on him, but he felt, no doubt, that he owed her nothing.

"Well, I think I'll go for a stroll," she said.

He watched her stretch her tall, slim body, standing first on one foot and then on the other. She had beautiful legs— quite perfect.

"Goodnight, then," she said.

She opened the French windows.

"Just a moment!"

He didn't know how to talk to her. She confused him. He felt sorry for her, and yet afraid of her, both at once.

She walked back, smiling too brightly. He couldn't think what to say.

105

"Were you thinking of coming with me?"

"Yes . . . at least, I was. But I mustn't, I've too much work. Good night."

He turned and began to walk upstairs, feeling uneasily that Danielle's eyes were following him. Halfway up he couldn't resist looking back: she hadn't moved, but was no longer smiling. He found her desperately beautiful at that moment, with her large green eyes, her full, red lips, and her thick, tawny hair shimmering in the bright light.

He went on staring at her, as if it was somehow necessary that he should. She showed no surprise, and when he began to mount the stairs again she called after him: "Good night, lover boy. Sweet dreams!"

He decided he had been right about her in the first place. She was vulgar and tedious.

He couldn't sleep. Lying in his pyjamas on top of the bed because it was too warm for him to bear any bedclothes at all, he chain-smoked, thinking of Louise, and of the risks they had taken earlier on. His old anxieties returned: he must go away, leave the Brassarts, stop working at the hospital, start again from scratch.

After switching off the bedside lamp, he turned over on his stomach and closed his eyes. He lay awake for a long time, and when at last he was falling asleep he suddenly sensed that there was someone else in the room. He remembered that he hadn't turned the key in the lock. So someone could have entered, and it was unlikely to be Louise since she had taken sleeping pills.

He turned over cautiously, and only just stifled a cry. A tall, bulky form in a white shirt was distinguishable in the semi-darkness. The figure kept curiously still and this stillness itself had a frightening quality.

"Keep quiet, Debosse, or you'll wake the entire household. Haven't you caused enough trouble already?"

"What do you want?"

"Put the light on, young man. I can't find the switch."

In the light, Brassart's appearance was distressing: there were bags under his eyes, his face was grey, his jaw sagged. He sat down heavily on the bed, and passed a weary hand across his sweating forehead.

Vincent was sitting up and was about to get out of bed when Brassart stopped him.

"Stay where you are, Debosse."

"Are you ill, sir?"

"Don't bother about my health, Debosse. Just tell me where you've put that blasted revolver."

"What revolver?"

Brassart stretched his big hands threateningly towards Vincent, who recoiled against the wall.

"I could wring your neck, Debosse, before you had time to shout for help. That would really be something to call the police about, wouldn't it?"

He was talking slowly and thickly, with the tedious over-carefulness of a drunk determined not to be interrupted.

"That revolver belongs to me," he went on. "Danielle Fellegrini stole it. It was she who was responsible for all that fuss. You remember? The night my wife thought someone had tried to kill her and you were in rather a tight corner. You know what I'm talking about, don't you?"

"It was Mademoiselle Fellegrini? How do you know?"

"I just know. Like I know all the rest. That you're my wife's lover, for instance. Do you think I'm a complete fool?"

"No, sir."

Vincent's voice was little more than a whisper.

"No, sir, yes, sir!" sneered Brassart. "You're a pious hypocrite, Debosse. I can't bear the sight of you."

"I've realized that, sir, and I intend to leave in the morning."

"You'll stay here, Debosse. That's an order."

"But, sir . . ."

"Don't try to understand. Just hand over that revolver."

"I haven't got it."

"Listen, Debosse, I know you have it. Mademoiselle Felle-grini, who is nearly as stupid as you, took the revolver to frighten my wife. She pushed the joke a little too far for your liking when she hid it in the pocket of your dressing-gown. You see, I know all about it. Come on, now. Hand it over!"

"I threw it down a drain, sir. You must believe me."

Brassart laughed loudly and then hiccuped.

"Down a drain, eh? Tell me, Debosse, is my wife good in bed? Oh, come now, don't blush! Tell me frankly—at least you owe me that. When she's in bed with you does she . . .?"

"Please, sir! You know I can't answer."

Vincent watched him wagging his head. "I'll kill him if he goes on like this," he thought. "I'll kill him. He's drunk and mad, too. But why hasn't anyone at the hospital noticed that he's gone out of his mind?"

"You can't answer because you're afraid of me, Debosse. But you weren't afraid of sleeping with my wife, were you?"

Abruptly, he fell silent, his expression vague and his face grey. Fearing he was going to be sick, Vincent stood up and took him by the arm.

"Come along, sir. Come out on the balcony, you'll feel better. The heat . . ."

But, with astonishing speed, Brassart grabbed his arm. Thrown off balance, Vincent fell back on the bed, and Brassart pinned him there with his whole weight.

"Let me go, sir! Let me go!"

Then he stopped protesting and tried only to turn his head towards the window and close his eyes to the frightening face bending over him.

"Tell me about my wife, Debosse! A subject we have in common, eh?"

He stank of drink. Vincent grimaced and remained silent.

"You little swine," muttered Brassart, pressing his beefy hands down on Vincent's thin chest. "When my wife's in your arms, you know what to say then, don't you? And you know how to make her . . ."

"You're hurting me, sir."

"I hope I am. I could go farther, Debosse. I could kill you."

"What are you waiting for, then?" said Vincent quietly.

Brassart's small eyes seemed to disappear in an ugly laugh. He relaxed his hold. Vincent slid to the floor, leaped up and sprang towards the window.

As he reached the balcony he glanced backwards over his shoulder and saw Brassart collapse on the bed. Cautiously he went back and saw that the man had fallen into a heavy, drunken stupor. It was a waste of time to try and rouse him or get him off the bed.

Vincent resigned himself to spending the rest of the night in the garden when he remembered that the old servant rose very early. She would certainly find it very odd for a guest of the Brassarts to be sleeping in the open air. There was only one solution: Brassart's own room. A fair exchange! "After all," he thought, looking back at Brassart who was now snoring, "if I can sleep with his wife, I can certainly sleep in his bed."

12

It was ten past ten in the evening when Commissaire Faure closed the file, leaving the last few sheets unread. He had smoked more than twenty cigarettes, eaten six peppermints, and drunk two glasses of water. He had also found the flaw he was looking for, but this didn't mean he was now able to arrest the murderer. He could see, in fact, that the real difficulties were only just beginning.

At ten-fifteen he rang Inspector Rageot and asked him to summon Vincent Debosse for questioning the next day. He spoke a few friendly words to the inspector, and then hung up. His last packet of cigarettes was empty. He had a headache and a queer sick feeling in his chest.

His wife. He hadn't had the courage to telephone her and she would never believe he had stayed so late at his office. God only knew what she was thinking! To throw off his sense of guilt, he decided that before the end of the month he would send her to Brittany with the children. He would rejoin them as soon as this damned case was finished. Then, after the holidays, if she was no better he would make her go to a psychiatrist.

Four children in five years. Perhaps it was that which had been too much for her. Four difficult children and a very young woman who had never succeeded in adapting herself to the maternal role. Yes, she must have treatment before it was too late. Apart from the Floride convertible, the only luxury he could offer her was a psychiatrist.

As he reopened the file, his telephone rang. He picked up

the receiver and his wife began shouting at him. She had been waiting for more than two hours. She had been worried to death. The children were unbearable. She would never forgive him. And so on, and so on.

He couldn't calm her down, and had to promise he would leave for home right away.

Vincent Debosse was sitting on the very edge of the chair, his shoulders hunched, and his hands clenched on his bony knees. When he spoke he stared at the commissaire's tie. His clear eyes expressed extraordinary mistrust.

Faure didn't consider Vincent Debosse as an individual. He had come across a number of young men like him—the type was only too common. They cared for nothing, gave nothing, and took nothing, not even a woman.

"Monsieur Debosse, I should like, if I may, to go back to the day before the crime. Right? Well now, we're at Chantilly, or to be exact *you* are at Chantilly. You have just seen Mademoiselle Fellegrini in Madame Brassart's room. You rush into the living room and there you find . . ."

"Danielle Fellegrini. I've told you that already. I've told you everything, my whole life story. Surely you aren't going to make me spend all my days at the *Sûreté*? I haven't much time to spare, as you know."

"Neither have I, Monsieur Debosse. But I have the impression that a lot of my time has been wasted . . . by you."

Vincent rubbed his damp hands on his trousers and took the cigarette that Faure offered him.

"What d'you mean? I don't understand."

"I'm the one who needs to understand, Monsieur Debosse. That's the problem. The only problem. So let's not waste any more time, eh?"

Commissaire Faure smiled a great deal. His fine, white teeth took people's minds off the sparseness of his hair and his protruding ears. But at this moment his face was closed, inscrutable.

"Monsieur Debosse, you say that, after seeing Mademoiselle

Fellegrini in the drawing-room, you went up to Madame Brassart's room to have a look round."

"That's right. Mademoiselle Fellegrini's behaviour worried me. I was living on my nerves. I was suspicious about everything. I was suddenly afraid . . ."

He was speaking in a quiet, tense voice, nervously pushing his hair back from his forehead.

"Afraid of what, Monsieur Debosse?"

"Listen, I'd been scared stiff by that business of the cyclopropane, and then the revolver. I wondered whether Mademoiselle Fellegrini hadn't perhaps put some dangerous contrivance in Madame Brassart's bedroom. I acted quite reasonably, didn't I? I went up and looked round, but I didn't find anything. That's all."

"No, that's not all."

Vincent turned very pale, but, for the first time, looked the commissaire straight in the eyes.

"I swear I . . ."

"Let's go back to your statement, Monsieur Debosse. You said that towards eight o'clock that evening, when the maid came to tell you dinner was served, you had the 'tormenting feeling'—these are your own words—of having forgotten something important."

"Yes, I did say that, but whatever it was I never remembered it."

"Monsieur Debosse, you have every appearance of being a very intelligent young man. You wouldn't be stupid enough deliberately to conceal some essential detail from me, would you?"

"I'm not concealing anything."

"Think carefully!"

"I'm not concealing anything," Vincent repeated. "Or if I am it's unconscious."

"Unconscious. You've found the right word, perhaps. When I reread your statement I had the clear impression that here was a young man who was indeed unconscious of the seriousness of his situation."

Vincent turned away to light another cigarette, and his long, delicate fingers trembled. When he faced the commissaire again there were tears in his eyes.

"This something important was in Madame Brassart's room, wasn't it?" demanded Faure.

"No. That's not true," protested Vincent. "You're quite wrong!"

He had raised his voice unexpectedly and Faure wondered whether this was because he was ashamed of his tears or because he was afraid.

"Please forgive me," said Vincent. "I'm absolutely worn out. I've been sleeping very badly, and I'm working very hard at the hospital. For the past few days I've been replacing a resident doctor who's on holiday."

"Monsieur Debosse, you're an acting resident doctor, aren't you?"

Vincent nodded.

"How long have you been operating?"

"You mean on my own?"

"Yes. How long have you had the responsibility for operations."

"About two months."

"Anything really serious?"

"No. Appendicitis, hernias, fractures. We call on the senior men for major operations."

"Monsieur Debosse, I believe your profession means a great deal to you?"

"Yes, it does."

"In fact, for you nothing else really matters?"

Vincent stirred uneasily in his chair but didn't answer.

"I asked you a question, Monsieur Debosse," said Faure. "Is it so difficult to answer?"

"It's a meaningless question. Other things matter, of course. But for me they're perhaps less important than they are for some people."

The commissaire sighed, seemed to hesitate, and then said suddenly: "Monsieur Debosse, what do you think of women in general?"

"In general, they don't interest me," replied Vincent spontaneously.

"You mean, I presume, that you are nevertheless capable of feeling love—or what is called love—for one particular woman?"

"I thought you would have realized that by now."

Faure appeared not to have heard. He was riffling through the file. Suddenly he stopped.

"Monsieur Debosse, I have several statements about you, including one from Mademoiselle Hélène Accard. Mademoiselle Accard appears to be very attached to you. However, on one point she seems to have no doubts. I quote: 'Vincent Debosse is incapable of love. It isn't that he chooses not to, he can't. Women don't interest him at all, nor men either, I may say. He's entirely engrossed in himself, in his dreams of becoming a great surgeon.' There you are. That's not all, but I'm not going to read every statement out to you. Let's just say that, in the main, all the people who have known you comment on your unscrupulous ambition."

Vincent shrugged.

"People don't like me. I've never had a real friend," he said simply.

"Why have you returned to the Place Malesherbes?"

"Because . . . because I've not been able to find suitable lodgings yet. The hotel where I lived for a week after Mademoiselle Fellegrini's death was too expensive."

"That seems rather a thin excuse, in the circumstances."

"It's good enough for me."

"You aren't afraid that it might appear a little . . . unseemly?"

"No. There's nothing unseemly about it. You're mistaken again."

"Perhaps you'd be good enough to put me right, then?"

Vincent sighed impatiently and looked at his watch.

"Look, I was told this interview would be brief. I'm due at the hospital very soon and I'm supposed to be on duty. I simply must . . ."

"Monsieur Debosse, I had hoped myself that this would be a brief interview. I had hoped that you would be intelligent enough to realize that it would be better to tell me the truth without any more delay."

"I've told you the truth."

"No, you haven't. And I could have a strict watch kept on you." Vincent smiled.

"You must take me for a child. I've appreciated your courtesy, and I'll even admit that it surprises me. I hadn't expected it. But I'm not naïve. If you had any evidence against me you wouldn't hesitate, you'd grab me . . ."

"In some ways, you *are* a child."

Faure had stood up and was staring non-committally at Vincent.

"Go back to your hospital duties, Monsieur Debosse. I'll see you again very soon. I hope that between now and our next meeting your memory will improve."

He held out his hand. Vincent touched it nervously, drawing back his own hand almost immediately. As he walked towards the door, the commissaire said abruptly: "I'll perhaps ask you to come to see me when Monsieur Brassart is here . . . but I'll think about that tomorrow."

Vincent turned abruptly, his face pale.

"You don't mean . . . isn't Monsieur Brassart still in the clinic at Neuilly?"

"He's coming out this evening."

"But that's crazy!"

"Monsieur Brassart is much better," said Faure, smiling. "His doctor is allowing him home for a few days."

"It's crazy!" repeated Vincent. "Brassart was in a very bad way when he went to the clinic. Neurosis as severe as that isn't cured in a fortnight."

"Monsieur Brassart is a man with a strong constitution—and a reasonable man. He wants to keep his children out of all this. He's going to see them tomorrow at their school before coming along here."

With his arms at his sides and his head bent, Vincent showed no further reaction. It was as if he was stunned.

"You seem a bit upset," said Faure. "What's the matter?"

"Nothing . . . nothing."

"Were you as upset as this on the day of the crime, Monsieur Debosse?"

"What do you mean?" said Vincent in a colourless voice.

The commissaire was sitting down now, absently flicking through the file again. He had remembered that he had a lot to do: he had to reconstruct the rest of the puzzle.

"I thought you were in a hurry, Monsieur Debosse. I don't want to detain you any further."

Before closing the door behind him, Vincent glanced back once more at the little commissaire who was so polite, who smiled so genially, and who was now apparently engrossed in his large file. He looked harmless enough.

As he examined his notes and the statements of the various witnesses, Faure was surprised to find that he had, in fact, very few details about the discovery of the body. But it was there that he should have found some clue.

May 25th. On that day a young woman who had been beautiful was found dead in her bedroom at Chantilly. Electrocuted.

Marthe, the old servant, was the first to become anxious. Mademoiselle Fellegrini hadn't yet come down for breakfast, her shutters were still closed, and her door was locked. Eleven o'clock. She usually got up much earlier. Was she ill?

Brassart, who was reading in his study, said that he knew nothing. Had anyone knocked on her door?

"Yes, Monsieur Brassart. I knocked several times. She didn't answer."

"Then she must be asleep. She must sleep like a log."

At midday, after some urging from Louise, Brassart resigned himself to taking action. He called Vincent and, one after the other, as they had seen in the cinema, they flung themselves against Danielle's door. It took five minutes to break it down.

Danielle Fellegrini was stretched out, not on the bed but on the tiled floor. She was wearing a short nightdress and her feet were bare. She had been dead for several hours.

"Don't come in!" Brassart cried. "Louise, go away."

She was hovering in the doorway. Vincent pushed her roughly back and stood in front of the door.

Brassart, crouching on the floor near the body of his mistress, which he didn't dare touch, looked like a large, demented ape. Danielle's hands were burned and her face was livid.

"Electrocuted. How stupid!" he said after a long silence. "It's too late obviously to do anything. Debosse, go and switch off the electricity," he added, standing up.

"We'd better call the police, sir."

"For God's sake, you'll see the police soon enough, Debosse, I promise you! But first of all, switch off the electricity. Do you want us all to go the same way?"

When Vincent came back, Brassart was standing in the middle of the room, hands in pockets, his eyes averted, more ill-at-ease than unhappy. He moved over to the bedside lamp.

"Look, Debosse! Come closer, for heaven's sake! Look! There's a bared wire next to the switch. That was presumably what caused her death. The electrical installations in this wretched house have always been neglected, and this idea of Louise's of having brass bedsteads in every bedroom—I was always against it!"

Vincent made a quick examination of the lamp and shrugged.

"All the same," he said, "it's a bit hard to swallow."

"What's hard to swallow, Debosse? Don't you read the newspapers? This sort of accident happens every day. It's an old lamp and no one ever thought to see if the flex was still all right."

"The flex is almost new. Anyone can see that."

Now it was Brassart's turn to shrug. He looked tired—very tired and old.

"Call the police, Debosse. I'll stay here. See that my wife doesn't come up; there's no need for her to be involved in all this."

As he was going downstairs, Vincent met Louise.

"Don't go up. She's dead. Electrocuted."

"But that's impossible, Vincent! She couldn't have done a thing like that."

He looked at her incredulously. Was she going to deny all the evidence on this occasion also? Would she invent some absurd explanation, drag in God knows what? He suddenly found her quite outrageous, and preferred not to answer.

He spoke on the telephone to a police sergeant, became entangled in unnecessary explanations, and said "thank you" three times before hanging up. He looked white and tense, as if he was going to be sick.

Marthe was standing by the telephone, looking terrified.

"They'll be here in a few minutes," he said. "They think they'll have to inform the *Sûreté Nationale*."

"Why is that, Monsieur Debosse?"

"I don't know, Marthe. It's dreadful to think of that girl lying dead up there for hours without our knowing."

"For hours? Are you sure, Monsieur Debosse?"

"It's obvious. She must have come back fairly late last night. We were all asleep, that's why we heard nothing. Anyway, she probably wasn't able to call out. I should imagine that when she went into her room she switched on the ceiling light first. That was safe enough. Then she must have gone into the dressing-room to undress. The clothes she was wearing yesterday are still there. Then she would have kicked off her shoes, put on her nightdress and gone back into the bedroom. The accident must have happened as she switched on the lamp. An almost unbelievable mishap."

He repeated all this a few minutes later to the police. He had been the last person to see Danielle Fellegrini alive. For this reason, the police officer—a plump, dark young man wearing an intelligent expression, which was misleading—concentrated upon him. He liked Vincent the more because Brassart had been replying in monosyllables, without ever looking at him. He didn't want to pester the great man—he thought it best to leave that to Inspector Rageot, who had just arrived—but Rageot obviously had no intention of pestering anyone then. To him the whole thing seemed crystal clear: a criminal circuit had been arranged in the victim's bedroom, and the murderer was almost certainly one of this motley crowd who had spent the night in the house. Rageot thought it best to behave circumspectly, and leave the pestering and the questioning till later.

"Who does the cleaning here?"

"I do," said Marthe. "My husband helps me with the heavy work."

Marthe's husband was there, too. He had put on a white shirt and a jacket to meet the police, and his wife had taken off her apron. Since her dress had no pockets, she didn't know what to do with her large, trembling hands. The old couple were both over seventy, and each had the same lined face and brilliant blue eyes. The man was bald and it seemed surprising that his wife was not.

No, they hadn't noticed anything. The room occupied by Mademoiselle Fellegrini was the children's room, but they came to Chantilly only once a month.

"How old are they?"

"Fifteen and thirteen," said Louise.

She added that they had come to Chantilly the previous week-end and that it was possible they had done something to the lamp. Boys of that age enjoyed tinkering with things.

"You call that 'tinkering with things', do you?" commented Rageot.

Louise smiled, surveying the pink-cheeked, self-important young man with curiosity.

They were in the living-room, and although Rageot had asked them all to sit down, no one except Brassart had done so.

Brassart seemed to be annoyed. He kept rubbing two fingers over his boxer's nose, and staring at his feet. When Rageot questioned him he replied without raising his head.

"Yes. I found the body."

"You were alone?"

"No. Vincent Debosse was with me."

The latter appeared ill-at-ease, but he made an effort to look the inspector in the eyes.

"Monsieur Debosse, when you entered the victim's room, did you notice anything unusual near the bed?"

This was the one moment when Brassart's face lit up, more with irony, than with amusement. "You see?" he seemed to be saying. "You see, Debosse, what these men are like? They ask you stupid questions and push you into giving even more stupid answers. You'll see."

"No, I didn't notice anything," answered Vincent, turning his back deliberately on Brassart. "I looked only at Mademoiselle Fellegrini's body. She looked terrible and she was dead. That was all I could take in. In any case, I didn't go over to the bed immediately. It was Monsieur Brassart who . . ."

Brassart stood up abruptly. He was an inch or two shorter than Inspector Rageot and as he made this discovery he seemed surprised and impressed.

"There was nothing unusual to notice," he said curtly.

"Not even two electric wires joined to the feet of the bed?"

Brassart lit a cigarette and waved the smoke away from his eyes.

"No, I didn't notice anything like that."

"Apart from Monsieur Debosse you were, however, the only person to go into Mademoiselle Fellegrini's room after her death?"

"Yes, but I don't see . . ."

"I went in, too."

Every head turned in the direction of Louise Brassart. She looked tranquilly from one to the other and added: "I can't see why that should surprise you."

"When exactly did you go into the room, Madame Brassart?" enquired Rageot.

"When Vincent Debosse had gone to telephone the police. The room was empty. My husband had just left it to go and change. Mademoiselle Fellegrini had been my guest. It was only polite to pay my last respects to her."

"Did you remain in the room for any length of time?"

"Barely a minute."

"And you noticed nothing unusual?"

Louise passed her tongue across her lips as if she was trying to repress a smile.

"Well, Mademoiselle Fellegrini's body was unusual in itself."

"Of course," said Rageot.

13

At the moment Commissaire Faure closed the Fellegrini file, Brassart alighted from a taxi in the Place Malesherbes, and Vincent Debosse dialled the Brassarts' telephone number from the porter's lodge at the hospital.

Louise answered very quickly. Her voice was low and she sounded anxious and afraid.

"Don't come, Vincent. He'll arrive any minute now."

"I can't leave you alone with him. He's capable of anything. He might . . ."

"He's here! I recognise his step. Please, don't come."

She hung up, but Vincent held on for a few seconds more. He was trembling from head to foot, and the porter, thinking he must be ill, stood aside to let him pass. At the door Vincent hesitated, then shut it behind him with a bang and strode quickly towards the spot where Louise's Dauphine was parked.

He would go to see Hélène Accard. He would tell her that everything had gone badly for him and that she had been right. When he went to live with the Brassarts he had fallen into a trap—and what a trap! He would tell her that the nice, harmless commissaire might succeed in understanding what had gone on, but that he, Vincent, didn't, couldn't, didn't want to. He'd go on refusing to understand as long as he could. He wasn't going to throw himself into that nice little man's smiling jaws, no matter how inoffensive he seemed.

He would tell her she was his only friend in this damned city, where he couldn't take a step without some woman chasing him. He would ask her to help him. He had no intention of leaving Paris—he wasn't going to budge—but he was ill, or at least he felt ill. He would ask to sleep in her bed, beside her, like a brother, and he wouldn't move; he'd be safe from the questions of the little commissaire, who was persecuting him.

Hélène lived in a maid's room on the sixth floor of an old house quite close to the Hotel de Ville. He had been there two or three times reluctantly, when he wanted her to do him some service. He knocked timidly at first, and then, when there was no reply, he began to hammer on the door with his fists. A middle-aged woman, a neighbour, came out on the landing and said that Mademoiselle Accard wasn't in. She usually came in very late and making all that hullabaloo wouldn't bring her back any sooner. Then she stood watching him suspiciously. He dropped his arms limply to his sides and stared at his feet despairingly.

The woman was still on the landing when he went downstairs again. He heard the church clock strike eight. The sky was overcast. He went into a café and drank a coffee, reliving the past fortnight. Despite the crime, despite Commissaire Faure and his tedious questions, they had been fourteen wonderful days: the two of them alone together in the flat in the Place Malesherbes. As soon as Brassart had entered the clinic in Neuilly, Vincent had left his hotel room to live with Louise. The little commissaire had suggested this was "unseemly".

Vincent smiled. Then, refusing to consider the consequences of what he was about to do, he went over to the telephone kiosk. He dialled the Brassarts' number three times, but there was no answer although he let the 'phone ring for a full minute each time.

It was only when he found himself in the street again, with the rain beating down, that he felt frightened once more. Brassart was capable of anything. He had said so to Louise, he had warned her. Now possibly it was too late.

He knew he wasn't yet a good enough driver to drive fast, but he did so all the same—jumping a red light, skidding round a bend—and ten minutes later he screeched to a halt in the Place

Malesherbes. An inexplicable feeling of anxiety prevented him from taking the lift. Out of breath and trembling, he reached the fifth floor landing, but hesitated before getting out his key. He might find Louise or Brassart dead behind the door. It would be madness to go in. He ought to get to hell out of it, praying that neither the other tenants nor the porter had seen him.

He walked down as far as the fourth floor, and then turned about, went up again, slid his key into the lock and went in, without switching on the light. For a long minute he stood still in the doorway, staring into the gloom, his hands clenched in his pockets. There seemed to be a mist in front of his eyes, he had difficulty in breathing, he felt as if he were standing on the edge of a precipice.

He groped forward. "I don't care if he does kill me. I'll be glad to have it settled. I can't go on like this." At last he reached the living-room. The curtains hadn't been drawn and the window catches were clacking as the wind blew hard outside. On the terrace, rain was glistening on the chairs and the whitewood table.

In the room, two chairs had been knocked over. Vincent stood them up and went over to the low table, near the settee, on which an opened packet of cigarettes was lying. In the ashtray he saw a lot of cigarette ends, the sort Brassart left. He wondered if there had been an argument here, and if afterwards they had gone out to dinner. Their cook had left them, and Marie now went home at six o'clock.

He remained for a minute or two with his eyes fixed on the settee, standing stock-still, trying to free himself from the paralysis of fear. His heart was pounding furiously. Gradually he became aware of an unusual sound, which he couldn't immediately identify.

It was the sound of footsteps. Someone was walking about in the flat. The noise was almost imperceptible, and seemed to come from the passage leading to the pantry.

His mind cleared suddenly. He moved quietly towards the end of the passage with outstretched hands, and after an interminable moment touched something soft. He only just managed not to scream. Then a bright light shone suddenly and he drew back.

She was leaning against the wall, scarcely recognizable. Her swollen face looked pathetic rather than comic. She was wearing only a dressing-gown, and was clutching the collar closely round her neck. Several seconds passed before the terror in her eyes died away, then she said in her soft, low voice: "Oh, Vincent!"

He put his arm gently round her waist and took her into her bedroom where she collapsed on the bed. Tears began to run down her cheeks. When he tried to take her in his arms, she flinched from his touch.

He removed her dressing-gown gently, and looked in horror at her delicate body. From shoulders to thighs it was black and blue and bleeding.

"What did he hit you with?"

"His belt. It was the buckle which hurt most. I must have fainted. When I came to he'd gone, and then, just now, I thought he'd come back. I wanted . . ."

"Don't talk about it, and don't try to move. I'm going to make you more comfortable."

It took him half an hour to clean her wounds and dress them.

"Your face isn't as badly hurt as I feared. In a few days you'll be all right. Did he use his fists?"

She nodded silently, and followed him with her eyes as he opened the chest-of-drawers, took out a muslin nightdress and tore the front from top to bottom. With this improvised wrap he covered Louise's body and then drew the sheet up gently. He lit a cigarette and looked at her without speaking.

"Is that easier now?" he asked eventually.

"It hardly hurts at all, but my head aches. Sit down beside me.

She took the aspirin he held out to her. "Sit down," she pleaded again.

He pulled an armchair near the bed, put out his cigarette and leaned towards her.

"Tell me what happened."

"It was very quick," she said, "but horrible. As soon as he

124

came in he started talking about you, but he was shouting so incoherently I couldn't really take in what he was saying. He was furious because I'd had you here while he was at the clinic. I didn't say anything. I just let him talk, and shout and stamp about like a lunatic. He kept banging into the furniture. We were in the living-room and Marie had just left. After a few minutes I'd had enough, and I went to my bedroom. He followed me. I tried to lock the door, but he pushed his way inside. That's when he hit me. First in the face. As I stepped back I tripped. He put his foot on me to hold me down and then he took off his belt. He was really foaming at the mouth, and his eyes looked wild and staring. He's mad. That's all."

"Do you think he'll come back?"

"He may have gone to the clinic again. It's possible, but I'm not really counting on it."

"If he comes back I'll be here," said Vincent.

She closed her eyes.

"You can't stay here all the time, Vincent. I'll have to leave. I must get away from Paris."

"That's not possible," he said gently. "You know very well. The commissaire . . ."

"The commissaire will understand. If I stay here Guillaume will kill me, like he killed that girl. He's a madman."

She looked very tired, on the edge of collapse. He murmured, as if to himself: "You'll have to tell your father."

She sat up, suddenly alert and almost aggressive.

"There's no question of that. I've told you a hundred times my father must be kept completely apart from my personal life. He's already terribly upset about the Fellegrini business. If he discovered, on top of that, that his son-in-law is nothing but a great brute . . ."

He looked at her without understanding, shaking his head, thinking "No, that isn't the problem, you're blinding yourself to reality again. Please be reasonable." But she was no longer paying any attention to him.

"My father simply mustn't know that Guillaume has attacked me," she said angrily.

Vincent exploded: "And when your husband has killed you, for Christ's sake, what is your father to be told then! You won't face reality, none of you. You see yourselves in a distorting mirror, but one day the mirror will break and you'll have to look at yourselves as you really are at last."

Louise smiled wanly, and held out her hand to him.

"Let's talk about it tomorrow, Vincent. I'm so tired. I think I could sleep now."

He leaned towards her, kissed her quickly on the forehead, and switched off the light.

He was a different person after seeing the bruises on Louise's body. He told himself that he was no longer afraid, not at least for himself. He knew now what he had to do and he would do it without discussing it with Louise.

"Are you going to stay with me?"

He nodded, forgetting they were now in darkness.

"Are you going away?"

There was such anguish in her voice. He took her hand again.

"No, I'll stay here. As soon as you're asleep I'll go and find something to eat in the kitchen and then come back. I'll put a mattress on the floor beside your bed."

She fell asleep very quickly, while he was still holding her hand and wondering whether he should ring Commissaire Faure immediately or wait until morning.

It was exhaustion rather than cowardice that made him give up the idea of ringing Faure that evening. For how long now had he slept for only three or four hours each night? He no longer knew. But from the moment he had thought of telephoning the commissaire he had felt drowsiness overcoming him irresistibly. He slept in the armchair he had pulled near the bed, his head lolling back, his mouth open, his breathing as regular as that of a contented child.

Towards six o'clock he woke up, stiff and chilled. Louise was sleeping soundly, lying on her stomach, her face buried in the pillow. He left the bedroom on tiptoe and went to the kitchen.

As he was waiting for the kettle to boil to make coffee, he

found himself thinking of his life at Asnières. The last years of a peaceful, undramatic existence, without any serious problems. A squalid life, he had always said, and he thought so still. He didn't want to return to it, despite the anxiety now gripping him which forced him to throw away the piece of bread he had begun to eat.

Since the *Internat* examination he had kept thinking that everything had gone wrong for him, and yet, through this strange plot in which he had been entangled, he had found love. He was living for the first time.

Four months. Those at least he had had. Four months of anguish and excitement, of fear and rebellion. Four months, nevertheless, in another world.

The coffee did him good. He drank several cups, leaning against the wall, a cigarette between his fingers. He went on thinking. He would wait until seven o'clock before ringing Faure at his home. He would explain the situation to him: Louise had been beaten up and injured by her husband. It might easily happen again. He would ask the commissaire to come to the Place Malesherbes, where he would make his statement.

In thinking of what he would say, he suddenly felt very cold despite the hot coffee, despite his thick dressing-gown. But this was the only way the situation could be resolved.

At six-thirty he took a shower, washed his hair, put on a clean shirt and the new, charcoal-grey suit that Louise had given him. He looked into Louise's room. She was still sleeping peacefully. He closed the door and went to the living-room.

At seven o'clock precisely he rang Commissaire Faure, who answered immediately.

They were in Vincent's room, conscious of the hum of the vacuum cleaner that the charwoman was pushing nonchalantly up and down the corridor. Faure had produced from his pocket a notebook with spiral binding and a ball-point pen. They were beside him on the bed where he was sitting.

Vincent sat opposite, stiff and upright on his chair. His hair was neatly combed, and his eyes surprisingly bright. He began to talk very quickly, as if he was suddenly afraid he might not have the courage to say it all.

"I want to go back to my first statement. I didn't exactly lie, but I did deliberately avoid telling you one important detail. In fact, it's of prime importance. You see, on the day of the crime, Monsieur Brassart went ahead of me into Mademoiselle Fellegrini's bedroom. He crouched down beside the body without touching it, and asked me to go and switch off the electricity at the mains. I hesitated, but since he was starting to shout I did as he asked. When I returned to the bedroom, he was putting something in his trouser pocket. A moment later he bent over the bedside lamp and I was able to see quite clearly what it was: two pieces of flex, the pieces you were unable to find."

Faure had placed his notebook on his knees, but he wasn't writing in it. He was tapping the blank page with the tip of his ball-point pen.

"Why did you not tell me this earlier, Monsieur Debosse?"

Vincent shrugged his shoulders and began to bite his thumbnail.

"It's understandable, isn't it? Brassart wasn't only my chief at the hospital—he had also invited me to live in his home."

"You're still living in his home."

"Yes, at a price! For his wife, anyhow. It was that business yesterday which decided me to talk. I can't understand why he was ever let out of the clinic."

"Don't worry about that. He went back last night. Tell me, what do you intend to do now?"

"What do I intend to do?"

"Yes. Are you thinking of continuing to live in the Place Malesherbes?"

"No. That would be 'unseemly', wouldn't it? I think I shall leave Paris. In the provinces I'd have better opportunities— from every point of view."

As he stood up to get the packet of cigarettes on the desk, he glanced at Faure and wondered why there was this odd pitying expression in the little commissaire's brown eyes.

"Monsieur Debosse, are you quite sure, this morning, that you have told me everything?"

Vincent sat down abruptly and tore open the packet of cigarettes.

"Listen, not only have I told you all I know, I've run considerable risks in doing so, I should think."

"Yes, indeed."

"What do you mean by that?"

Faure yawned politely, one hand in front of his mouth. Then he stood up.

"We must talk about this again later. But now I must see Madame Brassart."

"Why?"

"You ask such odd questions, Monsieur Debosse. I am going to see the extent of the injuries inflicted on Madame Brassart by her husband. Does that satisfy you?"

Vincent did not reply, but as the commissaire opened the door he sprang after him and said very quickly: "She must be warned. She's still in bed. She doesn't know you're here."

"I'll have myself announced, don't worry. The woman who opened the door to me can do that. Just rest for a bit, you look as if you needed it. I'll be back shortly."

His voice was calm, but the tone was as dry as the crack of a whip.

Vincent shut the door behind him, saying: "Fine. That's fine." But he looked less sure of himself than ever.

He had slept for an hour. Sleep had overwhelmed him, as if he'd been pole-axed. Now he was scarcely less exhausted than before, scarcely less pale.

He combed his hair in the bathroom, and told himself with some relief that Faure must have decided not to pursue his questioning. He must have left. In fact, the little man wasn't insensitive at all, he treated witnesses with consideration, never raising his voice. He had a gift that was rare indeed: he knew how to listen, to let people speak without interrupting them. He effaced himself and sat, silent, motionless, absorbed.

One thing was irritating: his concern for detail. When some apparently trivial point remained obscure, he would, with the same relentless courtesy, make you repeat the same story ten or twenty times.

Louise had said she had a high regard for Faure. She had treated his interrogations as a kind of game, particularly at the beginning. She said the little commissaire amused her, and whenever Vincent asked what had been said she answered: "Oh, just small talk between two well-bred people."

Had it been that kind of conversation again this morning? Suddenly Vincent felt alarmed. Why had Faure been so insistent that he must see Louise? And why had Louise not called him on the intercom as soon as the commissaire had left? Was it possible that the interview was still continuing and that perhaps . . . He panicked.

In the corridor he came upon a uniformed policeman. Dazed, he stepped back, but the man took no notice, continuing his patrol up and down in front of the main door, ignoring Vincent who slipped past him close to the wall.

In Louise's bedroom, Commissaire Faure, too, was walking up and down. At the sight of his face, both weary and relaxed, Vincent realized that this was the end. The presence of Inspector Rageot strengthened that conviction. He was standing in front of the window, large, at ease, a comic figure with his short, turned-up nose and his fat cheeks.

There was a silence. Vincent, who had remained on the threshold, tried in vain to catch Louise's eye. Her head was bent and she was looking down at her hands, which were pressed very firmly against her thighs. She was wearing the same dressing-gown as on the previous evening, and her pretty throat was hidden by a silk scarf. Although she was in her own bedroom, sitting on her own bed, she didn't seem to be at home. She seemed not to be herself. This wasn't Louise Brassart.

"Do you insist on staying, Monsieur Debosse?"

The commissaire's scathing tone of voice startled him. He walked into the room. Faure came towards him and took him by the elbow.

"I have something more to say to you. It would be better if you went back to your own room. Come along."

They were already in the corridor when Louise called out to Vincent in a voice he scarcely recognized. He turned about immediately, but Faure barred his path.

"Please, Monsieur Debosse, don't complicate matters. It is much better that you shouldn't see her again."

Standing in front of the window with his back towards the commissaire, he pressed his forehead against the glass, his eyes closed.

"Now there's nothing more that can happen to me. Now it really is all over."

The little commissaire had begun to talk a minute before. He had regained his usual suave, discreet voice. Between two sentences he sighed. Vincent was scarcely listening; the first words had been enough. Louise had confessed. Faure's comments were no longer of any importance.

"You made me waste a lot of time, Monsieur Debosse. Curiously enough, however, I don't bear you any grudge."

Vincent grunted and turned round sharply.

"After all, it was self-defence and you . . ."

"How can you argue that it was self-defence? I'm prepared to overlook the fact that you lied to me, but I'm not blind. In any case, from now on the whole matter is out of my hands."

Vincent smiled mirthlessly.

"I lied very little, in fact. All right, I know. The day of the crime, when I was in the garden, it wasn't Danielle Fellegrini I saw in Louise's bedroom. It was Louise herself."

"And that seemed all the more surprising to you because you had just seen her leave the house, eh? It was that little lie which put the whole investigation on the wrong tack. In fact, directly one knew that Madame Brassart was hiding from you the fact that she had returned to her bedroom, one had proof of her guilt."

"Not at all!"

"Do please face the facts, Monsieur Debosse. You were

afraid and you told a clumsy untruth. Think back: you said that you had seen Mademoiselle Fellegrini in Madame Brassart's bedroom, and at the same time admitted you had seen her reading in the living-room, barely ten seconds later. This little flaw made me reconsider everything. Let's take the facts chronologically. At the very moment when you thought she was out riding, Madame Brassart was re-entering the villa by the back door. She waited until Mademoiselle Fellegrini had settled down in the living-room before going to her bedroom and tampering with the electric circuit. Then she went into her own room to put away some of the things she had been using and saw you from the window. But she wasn't sure that you had seen her. So she went out of the house again by the back door and returned through the garden fifteen minutes later. Meanwhile you had gone to her bedroom, not to search it, as you said, but to ask her for an explanation. The room was empty, but you saw there a piece of wood beading which, in her haste, Madame Brassart had forgotten to hide away."

"At the time it seemed to me to be of no consequence."

"It worried you, however, because two hours later you had the feeling you had forgotten something important, remember?"

Vincent nodded, putting a clenched hand up to his mouth.

"Monsieur Debosse, as soon as Inspector Rageot spoke of a criminal circuit you knew it was the work of Madame Brassart, didn't you?"

"I wasn't quite sure. After all, Monsieur Brassart . . ."

"Monsieur Brassart himself understood immediately, believe me. He didn't suspect you for an instant. He hated you, but he remained objective enough to realize that you couldn't have killed Mademoiselle Fellegrini. And if he concealed the wire in question, it was certainly because he was convinced that only his wife could have been responsible for her death."

Vincent looked directly at Faure and leaned back against the Louis XVI desk.

"You can't persuade me that Brassart kept silent to protect his wife. He was thinking of his own safety, nothing more. By getting rid of the pieces of flex, he thought he could make it look like an accident and avoid a scandal. It was the same with the unsuccessful attempt to murder his wife. His objective was to avoid at any price having the police investigating his unsavoury affairs. He was no hero, you know."

He walked over to Faure who was sitting on the bed. "What's more, it was he, wasn't it, who was the first to talk? When did you see him?"

"Yesterday evening. He came to see me when he left here. He had to speak, Monsieur Debosse. What else could he do? The three of you had reached an impasse."

"He'd beaten up his wife—that was what brought him to an impasse. His jealousy made him speak, and when you arranged for him to be allowed out of the clinic, that was what you were expecting."

Faure smiled. He had no illusions. He offered Vincent a cigarette.

"Sit down, Monsieur Debosse, and don't upset yourself. I can't remember which poet said: 'Be a duster. Don't get mixed up with the table-napkins,' but you didn't take his advice. You got mixed up with the table-napkins, and now you're all mixed up. You see, the Brassarts' ethics are quite deplorable. They believe, quite literally, that they belong to a privileged class. Things that happen to common people can't be allowed to happen to them. You realize that Madame Brassart feels no remorse? She destroyed Mademoiselle Fellegrini because it looked as if her husband's mistress was going to be able to force a divorce on her, or, at the very least, to involve her in a scandal. And for Madame Brassart divorce and scandal are crimes more odious than murder."

Vincent looked down, his hair falling over his forehead, his arms crossed. The little man was probably right, but he couldn't yet accept the fact.

"I think you're mistaken," he muttered. "Brassart didn't want a divorce, and it would have taken more than Danielle Fellegrini to force him into it."

"The young woman was expecting a child," said Faure. "Madame Brassart knew that. She knew also that Mademoiselle

133

Fellegrini would go to any lengths to get her own way. Instead of telling the police, she preferred to take the law into her own hands. She was absolutely certain the murder would be thought an accident. Believe me, she never hesitated for a moment. She lived, as you know, in a world of her own. The day after the crime she volunteered the information that she had gone into the victim's room. It simply didn't occur to her that she was running any risk, that anyone could possibly suspect her."

"Did she . . . say anything about me?"

Faure hesitated. He remembered how she had broken down when she had spoken the young man's name. But could he believe her when she said she loved Vincent and had tried to protect him from her husband's hatred?

"No," he said firmly. "No. She made a very detailed confession. It was almost insolent in its candour. But no comments on anyone. I hope for her sake that her counsel will be able to prove that Mademoiselle Fellegrini made two attempts to kill her. For the moment we have only the somewhat unsatisfactory evidence that I found in Mademoiselle Fellegrini's private diary."

"Brassart could give evidence, too. He got Danielle to admit those two murder attempts. He couldn't possibly refuse to help his wife. He . . ."

Vincent broke off, disturbed by sounds coming from the lobby. Realizing that Louise was about to leave with Inspector Rageot and the uniformed policeman, he made to stand up, but Faure held him firmly by the arm.

"Don't go, Monsieur Debosse. You'd only make it more difficult for her. And for yourself," he added, with a sigh.

There was a silence. Then the commissaire went on quietly: "You have always got your career before anything else, haven't you? Well, then—this isn't the moment, if I may say so, to change your tactics. Forget Louise Brassart. You thought you loved her and . . ."

"If ever I start saying I *thought* I loved her, I'll be as big a bastard as the rest!"

He had tears in his eyes and his features were convulsed. He looked desperate, and yet, at the same time, somehow relieved.

Faure stood up, reflecting that eight years earlier he had said the same about the woman who was to become his wife. And today . . .

"I've someone waiting for me," he said. "I must go."

At the door he turned back: "What will you do now?" he asked.

"Pack my bag and get out," answered Vincent.

The mirror in the lift showed him a young man only a little paler, a little more melancholy than the one he knew. He looked, he thought, surprisingly like the tortured James Dean in East of Eden. The same extreme youth. The same unconscious self-dramatization.

As he crossed the large hall, he pretended—to forget that he still had tears in his eyes—that Hélène Accard might be there, waiting in front of the block, and that she would run to his arms. "This sort of story almost always ends that way," he thought, "whether in the cinema or in real life. The innocent young girl, disdained at the beginning, returns at the end to prove that the hero knows, at last, where true happiness lies."

But the Place Malesherbes was almost deserted, and, plainly, Hélène Accard wasn't waiting for him. With the back of one hand he brushed away his tears. He walked towards the *métro*. It was midsummer. It was raining. Life tasted foul.